STONE FURY

A Stone Cold Thriller

J. D. WESTON

ACKNOWLEDGMENTS

Authors are often portrayed as having very lonely work lives. There breeds a stereotypical image of reclusive authors talking only to their cat or dog and their editor, and living off cereal and brandy.

I beg to differ.

There is absolutely no way on the planet that this book could have been created to the standard it is without the help and support of Erica Bawden, Paul Weston, Danny Maguire, and Heather Draper. All of whom offered vital feedback during various drafts and supported me while I locked myself away and spoke to my imaginary dog, ate cereal and drank brandy.

The book was painstakingly edited by Ceri Savage, who continues to sit with me on Skype every week as we flesh out the series, and also threw in some amazing ideas.

To those named above, I am truly grateful.

J.D. Weston.

GET J.D.WESTON'S STARTER LIBRARY FOR FREE

Stay up to date with the Stone Cold Thriller series and get FREE eBooks sent straight to your inbox.

Details can be found at the end of this book.

1

CURTAINS

HARVEY STONE FOUND THE STAGE DOOR UNLOCKED AND slipped inside the old building; he closed the heavy wooden door softly behind him and let his eyes adjust to the soft light. Years of damp poisoned the air and a hundred years of debauchery had left a chill in the very core of the old theatre.

He heard the slap of bare feet running on the hard linoleum covered floor; the noise came from one of the corridors that led off from the main one where he stood.

Giggling girls were loud and shrill, and slamming doors boomed then hushed as another door slammed. He crept up the three steps in front of him and ducked into another side corridor to his right; this one was much shorter with fewer doors.

The wardrobe rooms were larger on this wing. It was meant for the big stars or celebrities, not the unknown extras, or dancers that filled the rest of the backstage rooms and probably shared one room between two or three. He heard the faint sound of applause somewhere far off behind many more heavy wooden doors. The show would be over soon.

He found the room that had been allocated to his target, wardrobe six. He slipped inside. The lights were on, and possessions lay sprawled across a makeup bench, with two lines of cocaine and a rolled up twenty-pound note in front of a large mirror that was lined with lights.

The room itself was divided into two by a temporary screen, the type that Marilyn Monroe or Rita Hayworth might have changed behind, way back when lines of coke and rolled up bank notes were only available to the wealthy and more successful performers.

Behind the screen was a small couch, cheap and stained from years of parties, makeup, alcohol, bodily fluids and general disregard. Next to it was a small table, on which sat what Harvey was looking for.

Harvey opened the laptop and was presented with a Windows login screen. He pulled a small transmitter from his pocket and inserted it into the USB port, then pushed the button on the ear-piece in his right ear, "It's in."

There was a crackle of static and then, "I see it."

Harvey watched as the laptop was remotely controlled. The password was found on the third attempt, and the controller was soon navigating through the laptop's hard drive. The controller found a maze of disorganised files, and ran an automatic search for MP4 files. Several showed up, and the thumbnails began to render and show.

"Bingo," said the controller over the comms. Harvey put a thumb drive into the laptop's second USB port. The navigator saw the external drive pop up window and copied the videos to it. Harvey removed the device and pocketed it.

"Switching to visual, the screen will go dark, but don't close the lid."

"Copy," said Harvey. The screen went blank; just the little LED next to the inbuilt webcam was lit.

Harvey had a look around. There was a large walk-in

wardrobe; pitch dark inside and empty of clothes. A small wash basin stood in the corner of the room, underneath which was a cupboard where Harvey found a few old rags presumably for cleaning, some disinfectant, ant killer and a toilet brush that looked like it was twenty years old.

He found a waste paper bin full of tissues, an empty wine bottle, and cigarette ash. Then he used a fresh tissue from the makeup table and wiped the two lines of coke into the bin. He tipped out some of the ant killer and racked up two identical lines of the white powder, chopping it finely to imitate the drug it replaced.

"What's going on, Stone? I can't see what you're doing," said the voice over the ear-piece.

Harvey didn't reply. He stepped back and studied his work, then slipped into the shadows of the wardrobe.

Harvey judged the wardrobe where he stood to be around eight-feet deep and five-feet wide. It smelled like years of musty disinfectant. He considered time. Applause, encore, then the maze of corridors. He estimated eight minutes from the applause he'd heard around six minutes ago. Harvey could wait. He'd waited in far worse places.

Screams and cheers came from the corridors as actors and actresses ran from the stage in celebrations of success, maybe even adrenaline. Who knows what emotions these people feel once they have finished a performance? More doors slammed, and more female voices approached, along with a male whose voice resonated through the old walls.

The door opened, and two people fell into the room. The girl came first and walked directly to the makeup table. She unfastened her costume jacket, it was brightly coloured, shiny and barely reached her hips. She slid out of her slender armaments and tossed it to the floor, revealing long gloves and a tight, bright red dress. The man closed the door with a flourish and danced to join her at the makeup table. He slid in behind her and ran his hands up her torso, then spun like only a professional dancer knows how, and began to unbutton his shirt.

"Did you see Julie in the final scene?" the girl asked him. "Here, help me."

The target stopped unbuttoning his own frilly shirt and helped the girl with the zipper on the back of her dress.

"I did, wasn't she wonderful?"

Harvey rolled his eyes.

"I thought the whole audience was going to simply burst into tears; she was so very convincing."

"That's what happens when daddy sends you off for private tuition, darling," the girl said in a mock aristocrat voice. She pulled her long gloves off her long arms and let the dress fall to the floor, then dumped the gloves on top, turned and admired herself in the mirror.

"Maybe this daddy could give you a little private tuition?" said the man as he stood behind her and joined her in the admiration. He ran his hands from her waist to her chest and cupped her breasts. He kissed her neck, softly at first, then harder; he began to grind himself into her.

"Maybe this little girl needs punishing? She didn't do any of her homework." She gave a naughty schoolgirl look, with one finger in her mouth, "Not. One. Bit." She accentuated each of the last three words by moving her hands inside to her hips. She finished by sliding her panties down to her ankles, pushing herself into the man as she bent over.

"Oh dear, Miss Norman. You have been a very, very bad girl indeed."

Harvey stood motionless in the dark while the charade played out before him.

"Wait," she said, as the man was pulling his costume trousers off. He tossed them onto the pile of clothes she had created.

She stood up and stepped over to the makeup table, picked up the rolled up bank note and expertly tightened the roll. Harvey had never been into drugs, but he'd been around them all his life. Drugs and crime went hand in hand for the most part.

She bent to snort one of Harvey's lines. Her pert chest bounced then hung as she leaned towards the table. She sniffed the line clean off the old wooden surface and passed the rolled up note to the man, who was now naked and keeping his less-than-impressive erection occupied while she was bent over. He took the note, and she dropped to her knees. He rolled the note tighter, and she took him in her mouth greedily. The man watched her for a moment, his eyes darted to the line, but he clearly didn't want to disturb her. Tough choice.

She coughed once then twice. The third time, she dry heaved and coughed again. A trickle of blood ran from her nose. Harvey had a clear view of it running, but she didn't, and he didn't.

She moaned as she took him all the way into her mouth then coughed and gagged once more. She pulled him away and saw the blood on him; a look of horror spread across her face. Then she fell to one side, supported herself with one arm and wiped away the blood from her nose. Her eyes widened in fear, and the dry heaving turned wet; a flood of blood fell from her mouth to her chest.

"Angie? What's wrong?" the man asked in a whiny, panicked tone. She looked up at him in shock. Struggling to breathe, she couldn't take in the air, but still dry heaved. She fell to the floor and rolled to her side. Her eyes remained open, and blood pooled from her mouth. It was quick but not painless.

The man bent down and grabbed her head; he slapped her face, "Angie, no, no, don't do this, come on, Angie." He looked around the room, "Shit, shit, shit." Then the realisation of the situation hit him. He stood and began to distance himself from her naked body. He stepped backward, he was panicking, and was about to make a fatal error.

He was three feet from Harvey, with his back to the dark wardrobe where Harvey waited.

Harvey held up the blade, ready to slice his throat if he came too close.

"Oscar? Are you coming?" a female voice from the other side of the door called.

"Come on, Oscar. We're heading to the bar for the after-party," said another girl.

"I'll, um, I'll be right there, I'll meet you there, at the bar."

"Well, don't be long."

"Apparently he won't be, not according to Angie anyway," the other girl sniggered, and the sounds of the two girls trailed off.

He stepped over to the makeup table and picked up the waste paper bin. He pulled a fresh tissue from the box on the side and was about to wipe the last line into the bin. He stopped, and dropped the basket to the floor; its contents scattered onto the old, dirty carpet. He picked up the rolled note from the floor and tightened it, bent down and snorted the line. He wiped the residual powder with his finger and rubbed it on his gums, then immediately spat it out.

"That a boy," said Harvey quietly, from the dark shadows of the wardrobe.

"Who's there?" said Oscar, as he dry-heaved and spat into the bin.

Harvey stepped from the shadows into the light.

"What the...Who the hell are you?"

The blood began to trickle.

"Who sets them up?"

"Who sets what up?" Oscar began to cover his modesty.

"I don't think you need to worry about covering yourself after what I just witnessed, Mr Shaw."

"I didn't do that, you saw? You saw what happened?" He coughed once, "She overdosed."

"You didn't do that, but you did this." Harvey held a flash drive up.

"What's that?" He coughed again; there was liquid in his throat.

"It's a video."

"Of what?" He wiped his nose, and a smear of blood ran across his wrist. He saw it and began to panic even more.

"It's a video of you and two hookers."

"So what," he coughed, "how do you know they're hookers anyway?"

"There's something special about these particular hookers though isn't there, Mr Shaw?"

Realisation spread across his panicked eyes.

"Oh god, I'm sorry, please help me. Call an ambulance."

"Tell me who set them up for you and I'll see what I can do."

He fell to his knees and coughed up a large amount of blood onto the floor.

"You want help, Mr Shaw? I can make the pain go away."

"Make it stop, make it stop," he cried, he was clutching his chest with one hand and holding his bleeding nose with the other.

"Tell me where I can find them, and I'll make it all go away."

"You bastard, help me."

"I can make the pain stop, or I can make it worse. You choose."

"There's a number," he coughed, and blood sprayed onto the floor in front of him.

"Where?"

"My phone, pass me my phone."

"What's his name?"

"I didn't save the number, but there's an SMS," he reached forwards and supported himself with one arm while clutching his chest. Blood hung from his face in a long string.

"I'm in his phone now," Harvey heard over the ear-piece, "I'm copying all the messages."

"How much did it cost you?" Harvey asked, casually.

"How much did what cost?"

The man looked up at Harvey; he was a mess. Harvey didn't reply.

"Fifty. Help me, god damn it."

Harvey didn't reply. The man looked up at him; shame etched all over his crooked face.

"Okay, each, it was fifty thousand each." His lungs failed, and he fought to take in air.

Harvey watched with wonder as Oscar Shaw; the infamous stage actor searched for breath; his final act. His eyes were wide and terrified. He fell forward onto the girl. Blood leaked from his mouth onto her stomach and ran, dark and sticky, across her skin.

Harvey placed the flash drive on the makeup table. He pushed the button on the receiver in his ear three times and left the room. He checked both ways but knew the supporting cast were nowhere to be seen; they were all in the bar less than ten minutes from curtains. He stepped out and walked casually along the corridor, jumped down the three steps and quietly opened the stage door. Checking both ways again, he dropped down into the alley below.

Pools of rain reflected the dirty back streets of London's West End, and the sounds of the busy streets in the distance brought a constant hum to the dark and otherwise quiet alley. He stepped around the puddles and clung to the shadows. As he reached the end of the alley, where street lights lit the ground, a black Audi pulled up. It stopped abruptly in front of Harvey. The passenger door swung open. Harvey barely broke stride, he climbed into the car and pulled the door closed. The car pulled away without any exchange of words.

2

THE LIGHT THAT SHINES

THE AUDI SPED THROUGH LONDON AS FAST AS THE SPEED limit allowed. They crossed the River Thames over Waterloo Bridge, neither Harvey or the driver, Denver, looked out at the Southbank which was lit up, its reflections spilling into the water.

Denver turned left off the bridge and followed the river downstream, crossing back to the north side through the Blackwall tunnel. Within ten minutes of being out the tunnel, they pulled up outside the headquarters of an unofficial, organised crime investigation unit. It was housed in a brick building adjacent to the Thames Barrier, and was a dark arm of SO10, the Met's covert operations unit.

The Thames Barrier itself was built in the eighties, and was designed to act as a flood protection system for the Greater London area; a series of mechanical barriers that open and close to control the flow of water in and out of London.

The unit was led by Frank Carver, who had led his team to success by capturing a crate of missing Heckler and Koch MP-5 sub-machine guns, taking out one of the leading organised crime families, killing a wanted murderer who had been on the run for more than thirty years and capturing a known sex offender who had missed his court appearance and been on the run. He had confessed to offences going back more than five years and eventually took the rap for seven victims.

The team was unofficial because the public simply couldn't know the team existed, let alone know about it being a dark ops unit. Many operatives of SO10 were not even aware of the team. While the unit was in its infancy, it would remain unofficial until such a time when its success gave the chief grounds for wider knowledge.

The HQ was situated perfectly next to the Thames for easy river access into London. The unit itself was shared with the team of engineers that managed the Thames Barrier. The building was far bigger than their needs required, and had been split into two separate departments specifically for the team. The barrier engineers were housed on one side of the building and Frank's team on the other; the two groups of people rarely met. The building was perfectly sized; there was a helipad on the roof, it was ten minutes from the Blackwall tunnel and fifteen minutes from the A406 and M11. Plus it was less than five minutes from London City Airport, where a small, used passenger jet had been seconded.

The large warehouse doors were slid open for Denver to pull inside without stopping. They were closed behind him by Reg, the tech guru. He'd been watching them on one of the twelve twenty-four inch screens that were mounted on the wall in front of his desk in, what he liked to call, his command station. His central screen had a game session open and paused, while the surrounding screens, which all connected to various servers and computers, showed maps, audio taps, video feeds, network health monitors and Reg's favourite medieval TV show. All of the devices that powered the screens were connected to a single KVM switch that allowed Reg to use just one keyboard and mouse to control the entire set up. It was the set up he had always dreamed of, and he had finished it off with a large, comfy, leather office chair.

Denver parked the Audi between the old VW Transporter, which served as the team's mobile unit, and Harvey's BMW motorcycle, in the small workshop area to the left of the large doors. The workshop comprised of three shoulder-height, snap-on tool chests which contained every tool Denver would need to maintain the vehicles, as well as an engine hoist, and an overhead hoist, which was fixed to a mobile gantry and large workbench. It was the set up that Denver had always dreamed of.

Denver was the team's engineer and mechanic. He was also a world-class rally-cross driver and pilot. Harvey saw through these talents and saw only a solid, reliable pair of hands. Denver had been given a choice as an adolescent, to either face prison for his multiple car thefts, or enter into the government's rehabilitation program. He'd selected option B and had since worked his way up through the ranks and departments.

Beside the workshop in the far left-hand corner was a caged off area that, according to Frank's strict instructions, was to be kept locked. No exceptions. The cage was twelve feet by twelve feet. Three of the four chain link walls had lockable steel armoury cabinets. The cage itself was Melody's domain, and she prided herself on her stock of weaponry and the cleanliness of her weapons.

Melody took credit for the operations of the team. She was a trained sniper and surveillance expert.

Beside the cage was Melody's desk. It was a simple set up with a laptop and a desktop printer. Next to her chair was a cabinet where she stored the surveillance equipment. In addition to the basic communications equipment, the team used the surveillance hardware because, if used correctly, it gave them eyes and ears wherever they needed them. All they had to do was plant them.

A mezzanine floor ran along the right-hand wall and across the back of the unit. Up there was Frank's office, a meeting room, a kitchen area and a mess.

Harvey had been allocated a space on the ground floor in the far right-hand corner, away from the large doors and beneath the mezzanine. It contained a punch-bag and a chair with a small table to one side. Harvey required few possessions.

Frank's office upstairs mirrored his previous office in the department on the Southbank which he'd occupied before he'd been offered the chance to head the new team. It was a fairly large room with windows opposite the door that looked out over the Thames Barrier. His desk was central to the room and two-thirds back from the door, with a large pin board behind it. The pin board was the only possession he had taken from his department office when the team had formed, and he had relocated.

On the pin board were photos of known organised crime families or groups. They were collated in various areas of the board according to the relationships amongst them. Some had a large cross drawn through them; some were linked to other groups with string. Six months ago Frank had managed to put three crosses through long-standing faces on the board. A personal best for one bust.

The analogy Frank used to describe being a cop of any description was that a city needs a method of disposing of garbage. If it doesn't have a method, the streets become dirty and hazardous. Society will never be garbage free because a new batch of garbage gets created even as the old one is being collected and taken out. Criminals are that garbage.

Frank heard the main doors slide open and the Audi's

heavy doors close. He heard the voice of Denver calling out to Reg, probably a childish insult.

Frank stepped out his office and leaned on the handrail. He looked down at his team.

"Stone, got a minute please?" His Scottish accent was soft and subtle and hid the underlying tone which meant that anyone he beckoned didn't know whether they should prepare for a bollocking or praise. It wasn't a deliberate trick on Frank's part. It was just his voice.

Harvey looked up from the workshop floor where he had just begun to fiddle with his motorbike's panniers and stood to walk towards the metal steps that ran alongside Reg's command centre.

"Close the door, Stone, take a seat."

Harvey did as instructed and stared at Frank. Harvey had a crop of dark hair, which was kept short at all times. He had an athletic build and stood at six foot one inch. He maintained a shaved face, but other than that he underwent no other grooming. The most striking feature of Harvey Stone was his presence. He had a way of telling you what you needed to say without moving his lips or uttering a word; a trait he had learned from his mentor, Julios.

Julios had taken Harvey on when he was very young. He had channelled the anger inside the boy and developed him into a killer. Harvey had been hunting the men who raped and killed his sister since he was twelve years old. The first man had been easy to find; he'd worked for Harvey's foster father. Julios had helped Harvey find him and take him out. Six months previously, Harvey had found the second man and tortured him, only to find out that Harvey's foster parents' real son, Donny, was the third man. Donny had been right under his nose all along but had fled to the Maldives following an attempt on his life.

Julios had been killed in the build-up to the event, which

left two people on Harvey's list. Donny Cartwright and the man that killed his mentor and friend, Julios.

The first lesson Julios had taught Harvey as a boy had been a simple one that he continued to practice in every element of his life. It was an art. Patience, planning, and execution. Harvey could wait. He'd find his target eventually. His executions were typically immaculate.

"Debrief?" said Frank.

"Debrief?" replied Harvey. "What do you want to know?"

"I sent you to do a job, so your debrief should be an account of the job's success level, plus any information on anything else that I need to know about."

"Shaw's dead," replied Harvey.

"Shaw is dead? That's your debrief?"

"I killed him. Well, technically, I allowed him to kill himself. I just didn't stop him."

"And I presume you didn't stop Angela Norman from killing herself either?"

"No, I didn't, that was interesting. I wasn't expecting her to show up."

"Interesting Stone? She was one of the country's most promising stage actresses. You let her die?"

"It would have compromised the investigation if I'd stopped her."

"Listen, Stone, I know you're new to all of this, but you need to remember you represent the other side of the law now. You're no longer a criminal. We have ways of conducting ourselves, and there are also ways we shouldn't conduct ourselves. Allowing an innocent actress to die is not one of the former. Is that understood?"

Harvey didn't reply.

"This isn't a bollocking, Stone."

"I don't care if it is a bollocking."

"This isn't a bollocking, but you do need to remember

that I have a file on you that would see you put away for more years than you have left in your body."

"Is that a threat?"

"No, Stone, it's not a threat, it's a demonstration of the lengths I had to go to keep you from being tossed into a six-by-four cell for the rest of your life. Have some respect. You're a talented man, Stone, but you don't intimidate me. You have an opportunity here to do a fantastic service to your country, repay some debts. Use it wisely. These opportunities are few and far between. Understood?"

"Repay some debts?"

"Yes repay some debts."

"You have a noose around my neck, and you're waiting for me to step out of line?"

"I *have* a noose around your neck, but I'd like to *help* you take it off."

Harvey just looked at him. He was neither angry or upset at Frank who was just doing a job for the government, and Harvey was doing a job for him, it was black and white.

"The bodies were found, the stage manager called it in around fifteen minutes ago. I don't have a full report yet; they're probably dusting for prints and running forensics. The only detail I have was that they were naked and looked like they drowned in their own blood." Franks' face turned into a look of disgust. Harvey remained impassive. "Why would they have drowned in their own blood?"

"That's what happens when you start messing around with drugs, Frank. Bad things happen."

"But why were they naked? What did you do to them?"

"They were naked of their own volition. They took drugs of their own volition. I just happened to switch their lines of coke for lines of something else. The unit is in the clear; there's no trace back to us. No cut throats, no torture, no gunshots."

"Good." Frank took a breath, "Listen, Stone. You're an asset to this unit. I want this to work, and I understand you're not used to the formalities, but I can help you there." Frank took a sip of water and watched Harvey's emotionless face, "In future, do you think we can work out a way of you giving me a debrief after each case? Without me having to chase you that is."

"Debrief?"

"Debrief."

"Reg has the number, there's your debrief."

"What number?"

"The number of the man who arranged the hookers for him."

Harvey left the room, and Frank shook his head in disbelief.

Harvey left the warehouse and took a walk down to the riverside, letting the cold breeze tug at his shirt and pimple his skin. He loved the river at night.

Harvey was still in a state of transition, and he was struggling. Up until six months ago, he had essentially been a hitman for his foster father's web of criminal activities. Now he worked for an informal arm of the very people he'd been avoiding his entire life. What a mess.

He walked down to the river and stared down at the water that flowed around the Thames Barrier leaving deadly whirlpools in its wake that would suck a man into the river's darkest depths. It was an endless cycle of power, always hungry always alive, and always moving, turning, churning.

John Cartwright had been just as hungry. Always planning a job, moving around, an endless cycle of power.

John Cartwright was Harvey's foster father. He and his wife Barb had taken Harvey and his elder sister on when they'd been left in his bar one night. Barb had wanted to foster them as they only had one son, Donny, and couldn't have more. When Harvey had inquired years later, he learned that his real parents had killed themselves in a double suicide and left a note inside the hamper Harvey was laying in.

John had always been surrounded by his men; his endless cycle of power. The men saw Harvey and his sister, Hannah, grow from babies. Julios, John's minder, had a soft spot for Harvey; he play-wrestled with him and taught him how to sneak and be quiet. Looking back, Harvey realised that the lessons in being quiet were more for Julios' sake.

Hannah was older by a few years and was developing into a young lady, much to the admiration of John's men. Harvey woke one night and found her bed empty. He had sneaked down the long and winding staircase into the kitchen, where he heard the violent whimpers and grunts of the men raping her coming from the basement.

Harvey had hidden in the shadows, he was just a boy, and saw only one man emerge from the basement. He remembered the man's profile in the moonlight like it had been scratched onto his eyes.

Less than a week later, Hannah had taken a kitchen knife and slaughtered herself in the night. Harvey had lost the only friend he'd had, and the only person he had truly loved. For her to do such a thing to herself was unthinkable. She'd been a happy girl until that night; she had shone.

Harvey had turned his grief into violence, viscously attacking bullies at school, and even hospitalising some of them. Eventually, John had to pull Harvey out of public school and invite private tutors to teach Harvey at their huge three-hundred-acre estate in Theydon Bois, Essex.

John had also asked his minder, Julios, to take Harvey under his wing and channel his aggression. Soon, Harvey was immersed in Julios' lessons. Self-defense and psychological control grew to incorporate martial arts, which Harvey absorbed. He began with defensive techniques, such as judo and aikido then progressed to taekwondo. Harvey was amazed at how Julios was able to simply side-step a punch and use the attacker's momentum to throw them to the floor, or disable a man using only one hand.

Less than a year into his studies, Harvey had adapted and taken on Julios' mantra: patience, planning, and execution. It was considered in every element of Harvey's life. It was around that time that Harvey had recognised the man whose profile was etched into his mind, the man from the kitchen on the night of the rape. He'd been one of John's men. Julios had understood Harvey's needs and guided him through his initiation.

Harvey had been patient. He had planned. He executed the man with just a blade.

He'd been twelve years old.

In the years to follow, Harvey and Julios became a cohesive team, carrying out the jobs for John that nobody else could do, mostly taking out rival gang members, or just sending a message to people that stood in John's way or on his turf. John had men to do dirty work, but often these jobs required a delicate touch, which was a little more refined than six guys kicking some doors in and opening fire.

Deep down, Harvey always had two things on his mind, two goals. Find his sister's rapist, and discover the truth about his parents.

He'd trained while he searched. For close to thirty years Harvey had been isolating targets. Sex offenders out on bail or released from prison. Scum. People that society wouldn't miss. He'd honed his skills in reconnaissance, surveillance, espionage and above all, he could kill somebody with his bare hands and had done many times.

He had become a force to be reckoned with, an incredibly gifted and ruthless killer.

Six months previous to the night Harvey looked down at

the water that swirled before the great Thames Barrier, Julios had been killed in a botched job organised by Sergio, John's adviser, accountant, and lawyer. In a turn of events, Harvey had learned that Sergio had been that second man; the man he'd been hunting for all of his adult life.

Harvey caught him and boiled him alive.

During his slow and painful death, Sergio had told Harvey of a third man in an attempt to let him live. The third man turned out to be Donny Cartwright, Harvey's foster brother.

Sergio's death had been horrible; he'd truly suffered exactly as Harvey had intended. But Harvey was thirty-two years old, and despite a life of dishing out justice, his own questions remained unanswered.

He was still unaware of his real parents' story, how they died, where they were buried. He didn't even know their names.

His best friend and mentor had been killed, but Harvey had never found the man that pulled the trigger.

Finally, his sister's death had not been fully avenged. Donny Cartwright was out there somewhere. Harvey would find him if it was the last thing he did.

Harvey had tapped out of the criminal world and rode his motorcycle to France to buy a small property and live out his days in the sunshine. Somewhere he could focus on finishing his life's work.

That's when Frank had stepped in.

Harvey's options had been slashed from endless possibilities down to just two; prison for the brutal murder of Sergio and anything else they could find on him, or turn his skills into good and work directly for Frank.

He sighed and stared out at the water. How it had all changed. He turned back and looked at the bleak brick building. It was a far cry from the little farm he'd bought on the south coast of France, twenty minutes walk to the Med, green fields and smiling faces.

Sure, he liked the team. They were okay, and Frank was okay too deep down. But the transition to the other side was difficult. The threat of prison loomed over him like a shadow on his heart. It wasn't the tough life of a category A prison that would keep Harvey awake, he could handle himself, and he was pretty sure that being who he was and being associated with John Cartwright would place him fairly high up whatever ladder there was to climb inside. But it was the knowledge that he'd never get a chance to find Donny, knowing that he'd never understand what actually happened to his parents, and never find out who killed Julios.

That's what would taunt him and keep him awake at night.

3

ABSENT WITHOUT LEAVE

FRANK STOOD AND WALKED TO THE LANDING OUTSIDE HIS office, "Mess room. Now. Everyone."

Denver had started to drain the oil from the VW Transporter. It was jacked up, and he was laying underneath removing the sump bolt, oil had begun flow into an empty container. "Great timing, boss," he muttered to himself.

Reg was leaning back in his reclining office chair. He had his wireless keyboard on his lap and was typing commands into a secure shell terminal that was hosted on a virtual computer in a data centre in St Petersburg, attempting to hack into his own systems. Lines of code filled two of the twelve screens. Each red line was followed by one blue line; attack and defence. His automated systems were working, but not fast enough. He was attempting to pull the resources from the firewalls with continuous attacks to prevent them from being able to operate efficiently. This particular denial of service attack would never allow a hacker inside the network, the attempts were too weak, but it would give the hacker an indication of the resources a network had so that he or she could tailor a more sophisticated approach.

"Reg, let's go," said Melody as she walked past. Melody Mills was five eight with dark hair and a cute exterior. She wore cargo pants, tan boots and a tight-fitting t-shirt. She was the little sister of the group but could hold her own in a physical or verbal confrontation.

Denver walked behind her wiping his hands on a rag. He had on overalls that were fairly clean and a baseball cap with the emblem of a little-known, British, high-performance car maker that he admired.

The four of them sat in the mess room which was around thirty feet long. One end had been arranged as a lounge with two dark-coloured, two-seater sofas, and a large TV on the wall. The end near the door had a dining table which doubled as a meeting table, with two large whiteboards hung on the wall behind the table. It was an efficient use of the space.

Reg sat on a sofa with his feet on the coffee table in front of the TV, which was turned off. Denver perched on the arm of a sofa while still wiping his hands with the rag. Melody stood near the coffee machine waiting for it to finish filling the pot. Harvey sat at the table. He didn't lean back, or forwards. He didn't make himself comfortable. He just sat upright and waited.

Frank walked into the room.

"Ah, we're all here, good," he began. Frank placed his files on the table and picked up a whiteboard marker, "We have a development in the human trafficking case."

The four all knew of the case and didn't react. Dead hookers turned up all the time, but the team had received other intelligence. Not only were girls being brought into the country to serve as hookers, but a certain gang were bringing them in and offering wealthy men the opportunity to torture, rape, hurt, and kill the woman in exchange for vast sums of money. Oscar Shaw had been one of those men.

"Reg, I believe *you* have the number of a possible lead? I

want to know who the number belongs to, and frequent numbers called and received."

"I can give you a location of the phone, plus SMS details and any email or service accounts that are associated with the phone."

"Perfect. Let's get as much as we can. Melody, please work with Reg to build up a profile. Once you have the name, I want his history and *any* information we can get on him, known associates, previous records, anything."

"It's probably a burner, sir," said Melody.

"Anything you can find."

"Denver, how's the fleet? We need to be in a position to move at a moment's notice."

"The fleet is good, sir. The Audi is brand new, and I've just replaced the exhaust and suspension on the VW. New wheels should be arriving any day now."

"How about inside?"

"Why don't I show you, I'm rather proud of it."

"Okay, I'll take a look when I come down." Frank smiled briefly. He knew that whatever Denver had done to the van would be impeccably over and above the team's requirements.

"Mills, as soon as Reg has a fix on the location of that phone, I need a recce. I need to see numbers, who's going in, who's coming out and who's not coming out."

"No problem, sir."

"Stone, work with Mills, you're going to need a way in. No drama, I need video feeds set up for Reg so we can take this down. We are *not* looking to take them all out. We need *arrests* not toe tags."

Harvey didn't respond.

"Right, get to it," finished Frank.

Melody left the room first, she was eager to get started on the surveillance equipment. Denver followed, eager to complete the oil change on the VW.

Reg followed and went directly to his desk. He used the virtual KVM switch and rotated the order of the screens. His security test was shifted to a higher screen, and an empty window was dragged into the central screen in front of him.

Harvey left the room last and walked back down the steps and past Reg.

"Got ya," Reg said to himself. Harvey stood behind him and watched him work. He saw the interface of Shaw's phone on Reg's centre screen.

"The number was in his messages, he said he didn't save it as a contact," said Harvey.

"Okay, so here's his messages. What's this one?" Reg opened a message from an unidentified number. The message read 'Thank you for last night, let's do it again sometime x.' "I'm guessing neither of the dead hookers sent him that."

"They're not dead hookers, Reg. They're the *victims* here, remember," Melody chimed in, defending Camp Female.

"Yep, right. Not hookers. Victims. Got ya." His eyes were blazing over the screen, he zipped in and out of messages and opened and closed threads, until, "Bingo." Reg switched the window to his left-hand screen and opened a new window on the centre screen. He typed a command, and a small program opened up with a search box in the top right corner. Reading the number from the phone, he typed it into the search box and hit enter.

The program ran some checks, and a progress bar showed up below the search. He sat back and breathed out sharply as if his work had been on a timer and he just beat the clock.

The search results began to show.

"Okay. The phone's last known location was here," Reg pointed and copied the GPS coordinates into the satellite imagery program, then dragged that into the right-hand screen in the centre row. He let the image render and turned his attention back to the phone.

"Okay, the last known callers are here, incoming up top, outgoing down below." He dragged the tab off to the screen next to the satellite imagery.

"Next, we have messages." Reg hummed a few bars of some indistinguishable tune, "Okay, let's put these here." He dragged the messages window next to the window with the callers.

"Now for the fun part."

"We have wildly different definitions of fun," said Harvey.

"That's why I'm the master technologist, sitting behind an array of hardware performing all manner of incredible things, and you're..."

"I'm Harvey Stone."

"That's right, Harvey. What *is* it you do for fun again?"

"That's a truth you're not ready for."

"Right." Reg sensed he had stepped too far.

"So?"

"So what?"

"So what's the *fun* part?"

"Ah, yeah, we know where he was last, we know who he's spoken to, and we know who's been messaging him. Now to find out who *he* is."

"This is the part where he finds out it's a burner," called Melody from across the room, "he won't be able to trace the owner.

"Ah, damn it."

"It's a burner?" asked Harvey.

"Yeah, untraceable."

"What about the numbers?"

"That's all we have to go on. Let's make it work."

"So you can search each number that the phone has been in contact with and come up with a list of names and locations?"

"Yeah, as long as they aren't burners too."

"Can you put a list of names together with a map of the owners' addresses or last known locations? We might be able to find a common denominator. Use that map as the central point and place the..."

"Customers?"

"Customers around that location. We'll build a web."

Melody had walked behind them both and was looking at the collation of the data.

"That's a *great* idea," she said.

Harvey turned but didn't reply. He acknowledged her comment with the slightest of nods and turned back to the screens.

The satellite image showing the phone's location had finished rendering. The image showed a spot in the Essex suburbs outside East London. Reg zoomed into the location and found a small cluster of buildings off Pudding Lane near Hainault.

"Essex countryside, Reg. It's rife with crime."

"Apparently so," replied Reg. They were referring to the bust that had landed Frank and his team with the new dark ops unit. It had happened at Harvey's foster father's converted farmhouse, which was also in the Essex countryside. Harvey had tortured and killed Sergio, and had left a wanted sex offender and twelve missing Heckler and Koch MP-5 sub-machine guns for the police to find.

"Okay we have a location, Melody," said Reg.

"Send it through to me," she said, walking back to her desk.

"On its way, now let's put some faces to some numbers."

"Last caller was one Mr Shaw, would you believe it? Next, we have a Barnaby Brayethwait, cool name."

"Can we run a match on any common numbers between them?"

"That's happening as we speak. Right, next we have a Mr Cartwright, Donald."

Harvey was looking at the profile of Barnaby Brayethwait on the left-hand screen when the name registered.

"*Stop.*"

"What's up?" asked Reg.

"That last name."

Reg read it off the screen again, "Mr Cartwright, Donald."

"Find me the location of that number."

"Well yeah I can do, but I'm building a database here, as soon as we've been-"

"Stop the database, find me the location of that number."

Melody heard the tension and rose from her desk. She began to walk over. Harvey stepped across to his bike and pulled his leather jacket from the handlebars.

The satellite image began to render as Harvey walked back to Reg.

"What's happening here?" asked Melody.

"How recent is this location?" asked Harvey pulling his helmet on and ignoring Melody.

"It's live, he's there now."

The image showed the exact same location as the burner.

"Harvey?" asked Melody.

He swung his leg over his bike then turned to her. "There's something I need to do," he said as he turned the key in the ignition and nodded at Reg to open the doors.

4

THE ONE THAT GOT AWAY

HARVEY FELT THE CONSTANT VIBRATION OF HIS PHONE IN his inside jacket pocket during the thirty-minute ride to the spot where the satellite image had shown Donny to have been. Harvey pulled into the car park of a nearby pub called the Maypole to stop and deal with the team. He wanted an update from Reg anyway.

He called Reg's phone.

"You alone?" he asked as soon as Reg answered.

"The whole team is here, you're on loudspeaker," Reg replied.

"Donald Cartwright, what's his location?"

"It's not as easy as that, Stone." It was Carver. "You don't get to run free and take care of your own personal projects, especially when they compromise the entire case."

They was a long silence, then, "I *need* to do this," said Harvey.

"You're either with us or against us, Stone. There is no half-way point."

Harvey didn't reply.

"You come back now and we can work this case together, you might even help us arrest your brother."

"Foster brother."

"Well, like I said. If you choose to go your own way, you'll be on the ten most wanted list in under an hour, and every cop in the country will be onto you. I can't have rogue agents, Stone. I can't just *watch* you go after a known suspect. We need the man behind the operation, the source, and that isn't Donny."

Harvey didn't reply.

"Harvey, what d'ya say? Come on back, and let's do this together. We want you in this team."

"I can't. I need to do this."

Harvey disconnected the call and pocketed the phone. He pulled his helmet back on, then turned right out of the car park. He took the turn into Pudding Lane three hundred yards later and rode slowly along the quiet, narrow road. Harvey knew the lane well and knew the group of buildings he had seen on the satellite image. The area used to be a large farm which had been divided into smaller plots and bought out. The buildings had been converted into small business units over the years and were now independent of the farmland that surrounded them. Harvey took a slow ride and approached the long driveway.

He had no intention of entering the property but instead wanted to get a lay of the land. He needed somewhere close by so he could park up and wait for Donny. The buildings were four hundred yards away. He could see a few cars parked outside them. One of them, in particular, caught his attention. It looked like a black Mercedes. Donny had had a black Mercedes before. Back when they were brothers, back when Julios was alive. He rode on slowly and found a turn off that led nowhere, it was two hundred metres past the entrance to the old farm on the opposite side of Pudding Lane. He pulled in and turned off his engine, then removed his helmet and considered the move he'd just made.

He was torn. Part of him had enjoyed working with Frank and the team. It was structured and organised and played to Harvey's methodology. A large part of him had, however, longed for freedom. He'd never actually got to enjoy the place he'd bought in France, Frank had caught up with him within a week and laid the options on the table. Go to work for him and put his skills to good use, or go to prison for a very long time.

Harvey had spent his entire life doing two things. Working for his criminal foster father, John Cartwright, and hunting the man that had raped and killed his sister. Donny Cartwright.

Donny was now less than a mile away. He could just walk in there and wring his neck but knew that Reg and the team would be tracking him, watching his every move. He would be taken down before he could get away. Besides, the death would be too quick, the scenario left no room for suffering, and Donny needed to suffer. No, it was best to just follow Donny to see where he lived and what his habits were; take the fight away from the scene. Patience and planning.

Donny would be treated the same way as Harvey's targets had been; using Julios' methods. Harvey knew that they were the key to success. During the years he had been hunting for Sergio, Harvey had honed his hunting skills on known predators. The media always announced them one way or another. Harvey had cleansed the world of thirty-three sex offenders. The number would have been thirty-four, but he'd donated the last one to the law when he made his escape to France. Frank had claimed that victory when he'd walked in and found the boiled remains of Sergio along with a recorded audio confession from them both.

The black Mercedes cruised passed the turnout where

Harvey was parked. Harvey pulled his helmet on, started the bike and pulled to the end of the road. A silver Nissan SUV was directly behind Donny, which worked in Harvey's favour as Donny would recognise the bike and the rider in his mirror.

He followed the cars at a distance for fifteen minutes then, when Donny turned into an underground car park of a swanky looking apartment block, Harvey prepared to carry on straight without stopping, but the Nissan pulled into the car park behind the Mercedes. They were together. Harvey rode on.

Stopping at a petrol station, he ordered a salt beef and mustard bagel from the sandwich counter inside. It was more to pass the time than to quench any grumblings of his stomach, and Harvey didn't know when he would next eat.

Harvey gave Donny and his accomplice time to settle in while he developed a plan in his head. The best plans were developed in his head over time, which he was rapidly running out of.

His bike was recognisable to Donny; he needed something he could get closer with. The team's Audi would have been ideal.

He was sat in a side street, hidden from passing cars while he ate with his helmet off. Pulling his phone from his pocket, he ran a search for Barnaby Brayethwait. Harvey preferred to use a secure VPN when performing searches on targets, but needs must.

There were a surprising amount of Barnaby Brayethwaits. According to the search engine, one was a plumber in Manchester, another a musician, and then he found the man he was looking for. Barnaby Brayethwait was a local Labour MP. He looked to be mid-fifties, slightly overweight, with a full head of thick grey hair and a false smile. He was definitely a politician.

Harvey thought about finding him. He no longer had the luxury of time, a laptop and Reg's resources. Running a search for Brayethwait's name and address would leave a direct trail to Harvey's phone, which was linked to the unit and would compromise the team. He hated that he thought that way. Was he turning?

Instead, he searched for the Chigwell Labour office and found the jurisdiction fell under Redbridge. The website pointed him to Epping, where the office was based. He made a mental note of the address and shut down the search.

It was getting late, the office would be closed, and Harvey needed to think. He found an Airbnb nearby and got his head down. It wasn't ideal, and the lady was slightly put off when she showed him the room and he closed the door on her without so much as a thanks. He showered in the en-suite and lay on the cool sheets. His Sig lay next to him on the bed. His clothes were neatly piled on a chair and his leather jacket hung on the back. He stared at the ceiling, planning.

Frank had finished the briefing and returned to his office to mull over the potential flaws in the plan. He often did this while the team carried out research and prepared, and created a list of potentials that would question the integrity of the plan they devised.

He heard the shutter doors open and Harvey's bike start, so he rose and went to stand at the handrail.

Harvey was sitting on his bike. Melody stood nervously watching him, and Reg reluctantly opened the doors. There was a tension in the room. He was about to call out when Harvey revved the engine and rode out of the unit.

Reg closed the doors behind him.

"What just happened?" Frank asked.

Melody turned in surprise and looked up at him, "Harvey, sir. He just left."

"Yeah I saw that, but why? Where's he going? What's going on?"

Reg Tenant sat back in his chair and began to pull up LUCY on the central screen. LUCY was Reg's own creation. It was a combined hardware and software solution that, among other functions, monitored the satellite & GPS tags that he had planted on all of the team. They all knew about the chips in the vehicles and phones, except Harvey, it was a security protocol Frank has instructed Reg to carry out in case Harvey disappeared.

Reg had built and developed LUCY himself. The system was an extremely powerful software and hardware solution that, officially, stood for Location and Unilateral Communication Interface, or LUCI. However, Reg preferred the unofficial name of Lets Us Catch You, so she had been christened LUCY and, in Reg's eyes, had a full personality.

As far as hardware, LUCY was a combination of four servers, one master and three slaves. Each server contained twenty-four multi-core processors plus one hundred and twenty-eight gigabytes of memory.

LUCY's interface ran on a virtual operating system so that if ever the system crashed, a new instance would fire up on a slave server to ensure continuity and zero downtime.

The database was striped across several block-level storage systems, with a combined storage potential of one hundred and twenty-eight petabytes, in a RAID one plus zero configuration.

LUCY was powered by one high-powered, uninterruptible power supply, with three identical UPS in passive mode. Beyond the UPS power, a backup generator stood ready to kick in.

LUCY's capabilities included the ability for Reg to view

and manage multiple pieces of software to provide a single view for satellite imagery. He could then identify the location, speed, height above sea-level and temperature of the digital tracking chips that allowed Reg to monitor the team and suspects.

In addition to the tracking chips, which were just five millimetres square, LUCY had the ability to monitor mobile phones on virtually any network internationally. This allowed Reg to not only hear the conversations but access a live view of a smart phone's interface, which provided access to messages, calendars, contacts and more.

LUCY also managed the comms system the team used on operations. Tiny ear-pieces were worn by the team that linked with the headquarters using various communication methods, including VHF radio. The ear-pieces had a tiny button for push-to-talk, or, if the operative wanted to open the comms, they could keep the button pushed in for two seconds, and the channel would remain open. Anybody else on the encrypted comms system would hear everything.

Through LUCY, Reg could group the tiny chips, and assign a particular group to a particular person. Once assigned, habits were monitored, patterns were analysed, and the information was stored in a database to be called upon faster than manually identifying trends in the individual's habits. He could even set alerts that identified if a person being tracked deviated from their usual habits. He knew that Melody visited Starbucks every morning without fail. When she didn't get a coffee one morning and drove straight to HQ, Reg asked her if Starbucks had been closed, which freaked her out; and she'd told him so.

"Tenant, show me-"

"Already on it, sir."

He browsed the groups in the directory tree on the left of the window and expended the view to find Harvey. Harvey had four chips. His phone, his bike, his leather jacket and his wristwatch. The wristwatch had been the hardest to plant, as Harvey only ever took it off when he trained, and even then it was in clear view. If Harvey had caught him, he imagined the consequences to be quite severe to Reg's own health. But he had pulled it off with the help of Frank, who had called Harvey to his office while he was beating the crap out of his punch bag.

LUCY dialled in on Harvey. All four chips were travelling at seventy miles per hour on the A406 North Circular Road. They watched as the speed reduced every now and then as Harvey slowed for the speed cameras. They watched him all the way.

They said nothing, but the tension grew as Harvey drew closer to Pudding Lane. When he was coming through Hainault, Frank said, "Get him on the phone."

Reg used the on-screen digital phone application to dial Harvey's number, he routed the audio through the speakers and mic that he used to communicate with the team through their ear-pieces.

The call rang out, and a woman's voice told them that the number they had dialled had not responded.

"Again," said Frank.

Reg tried again. On the third attempt, they saw the bike slow and stop in a pub car park at the top of Pudding Lane. The call rang out again, and once more they heard the dull tones of the woman telling them that the number they dialled had not responded.

"One more time," said Frank, "Denver, is that van ready?"

"Wait," said Melody, "he'll call us, on his terms. Just wait."

Reg's audio system started to play the default ringtone through his speakers.

"You alone?" asked Harvey.

"The whole team is here, you're on loudspeaker," Reg replied.

"Donald Cartwright, what's his location?"

Frank stepped closer to the screens, though he couldn't see a microphone, he spoke loud and clear, "It's not as easy as that, Stone, you don't get to run free and take care of your own personal projects, especially when they compromise the entire case."

Frank turned to Melody who nodded.

"I need to do this," said Harvey.

"You're either with us or against us, Stone. There is no half-way point."

Harvey didn't reply.

Frank pushed a little harder, "You come back now, and we can work this case together, you might even help us arrest your brother."

"Foster brother," Harvey reminded him.

"Well, like I said. If you choose to go your own way, you'll be on the ten most wanted list in under an hour, and every cop in the country will be onto you. I can't have rogue agents, Stone. I can't just watch you go after a known suspect. We need the man behind the operation, and that isn't Donny."

Harvey didn't reply.

Frank pushed again, "Harvey, what d'ya say? Come on back, and let's do this together. We want you in this team."

"I can't. I need to do this." He disconnected the call.

"Shall I call back?" asked Reg.

"No," said Melody, "that's enough for now."

Denver had joined the rest of the team at Reg's workstation. "The van will be another hour, I'm halfway through an oil change."

"Okay, finish it fast. The three of you are going on a recce. Mills, surveillance. Tenant, LUCY and comms. Load the van now, you're out of here as soon as Cox is finished." Frank turned to walk up the steps.

Reg had a flight case with everything he needed inside. It was ready on the floor by his desk, along with a large sports bag. He continued to watch Harvey.

Harvey seemed to be parked up in a dead end turning passed the entrance to the old farm. Reg hit refresh on the satellite imagery of Donald Cartwright's phone. Cartwright was still at the location. Then the icon began to move across the screen.

"Wait, Cartwright is on the move."

Frank turned and joined him again. They watched as Donny drove past Harvey and Harvey began to follow him at a distance. The screen looked like a cheap eighties video game.

When Donny's phone lost its signal, Harvey continued on for another mile, then stopped at a petrol station.

"What's he *doing*, Tenant?" asked Frank.

"Not sure, sir. Did he see Cartwright turn, or was he too far behind?" he set an alert to sound when Harvey's phone was unlocked so he could monitor his phone.

"Harvey wouldn't be too far behind. He's a pro," said Frank admiringly.

Five minutes later, LUCY announced activity on Harvey's phone. Reg hit the green *Voyeur* button he had created, and the display on Harvey's phone appeared on Reg's screen. They watched Harvey search for Barnaby Brayethwait.

"Barnaby Brayethwait?" said Frank.

"Second name on the list, sir. He messaged the suspect's phone shortly after Donny. I read his name out before Cartwright's, Harvey must have remembered his name and is looking for another way in."

"Mills, get me everything you can on this Barnaby guy. What's he doing Tenant?"

"Well, sir. The average bloke would just search for the name and the accompanying address, but Harvey-"

"*Isn't* the average guy is he?" finished Frank.

They watched Harvey search instead for the local Labour office, and the address of the Epping office came up on Harvey's phone.

"Barnaby Brayethwait. Fifty-three. Local Labour MP for Redbridge Labour, been voted in three years running. Divorced, two children, one seventeen and one twenty, both girls. The girls both live with his ex-wife in Walthamstow, E17. He lives on his own in Upminster, Essex. Drives a blue BMW M3."

"What time does he finish work?"

"No time stated, but the office closes at three pm, presumably if he's been voted in three years running, he's not the type to cut out early."

"But he is apparently the type to visit an illegal brothel and murder a prostitute?"

"Just not in working hours, sir," remarked Reg, with a smile that faded as Frank's glare grew.

"Harvey's not hitting him tonight," said Melody.

Frank followed her eyes back to the screens. Harvey was searching for an Airbnb.

"Good. He'll hit him tomorrow morning and you three will be there to make sure nothing goes wrong," said Frank, as he turned to walk up the steps.

5

EVEN MONSTERS CRY

HARVEY LEFT THE AIRBNB WHERE HE'D STAYED EARLY. He'd showered again, and dressed in the same clothes. On the ride from Chigwell to Epping, he took a twenty-minute slow cruise through the lanes. It was a fresh morning, and the sun rose behind a blanket of clouds as he made his way through the winding roads.

The high street was growing busy with the early morning traffic. People walked to the train station with their hands stuffed deep into their pockets, their heads down, and their chins tucked into the neck of their coats or scarves.

Harvey knew the street where the Labour office was; he didn't need to do a recce. It was one of the main roads out of town, so he drove instead to the coffee shop that he and Julios had once used for their meets. The coffee shop was warm inside; he chose a seat by the window with his back to the wall. Old habits.

He didn't recognise the waitress, it had been six months since he was last there. While waiting for his coffee, he went over his plan in his head. He would park up near the Labour office and check the Barnaby guy out when he arrived to work. It wasn't much of a plan, but it was early doors and ideas were brewing.

His original plan had been to wait for Barnaby to finish work and follow him home, then Harvey would have more time to extract the information he was looking for. But time wasn't on his side, the team would be following his every move. So Harvey made the evening option plan B and moved onto the morning option, plan A, which was more brutal and would be more effective.

At seven thirty am, he made his way to the offices, looking for somewhere inconspicuous to park his bike. Finding a discreet spot on the pavement, Harvey tucked his helmet into the motorbike's back box, locked it and strode off on foot towards the Labour office car park. He found a suitable place to stand and wait, mimicking a man waiting for a ride to work.

Barnaby was the MP for the area; he would wear a suit to work and probably drive a nice car. A Mini pulled into the car park. Not him, too small. A man of Brayethwait's stature would drive a large four-door, less than three years old.

Several more cars arrived, only one of which was a possibility but was driven by an Asian man. Harvey was patient. He didn't question his plan.

The entrance to the car park was a small alleyway between the office and the next building. There were no gates that would close and lock, only a parking metre. Presumably, the workers would have some sort of method to get discounted parking. Harvey wasn't sure. He'd never had a real job. His work with Frank was his first real job, and it wasn't really a job. The unit didn't pay him directly. He didn't have a National Insurance number and hadn't been seen by any authorities before. Frank was able to move money located to the unit's consumable requirements to pay Harvey, and he was lucky to get that. He could be earning five pounds a week mopping the floor in Pentonville.

Harvey stood at the front of the building on the main road. He watched the traffic drive past; buses full of school kids and minivans driven by tired mums. Men walked briskly along, most people didn't even notice Harvey. People were often like that. They don't see what they aren't looking for. Harvey was the opposite. He saw what he wasn't looking for. So when the blue BMW pulled off the main road into the car park, not only did Harvey catch the face of Barnaby Brayethwait, but he caught the shape of the VW Transporter that had pulled over two hundred yards away. He pushed off the wall and followed the BMW into the car park. Before Barnaby had a chance to open his driver's door, Harvey casually opened the passenger's side and climbed in.

"Drive."

"What the-"

"No questions, drive, you're in danger."

"Who are you?"

"Just drive Mr Brayethwait, I'm an associate of Mr Cartwright."

"Donny?"

"Just drive, no time for questions now." Barnaby had just announced his involvement.

"This is most-"

"This is the last time I'm going to tell you, put the car in gear, and drive. Turn right out of the car park."

Barnaby did as he was told; his hands had begun to shake and he fumbled with the double clutch gear box.

"You're going to tell me who-"

"You're right, I am going to explain everything. For now, just drive."

Barnaby took his phone from his pocket and began to search for a recent number.

Harvey reached across and took the phone from him. He wound the window down and tossed the phone into a refuse truck.

"What the hell are–"

"Shut up, Mr Brayethwait." Harvey raised his voice, and Barnaby was silenced. "You do not call the shots here. You do not ask questions. If you want to live until lunchtime, I suggest you keep your mouth closed. Take the next right."

Barnaby was taken aback but made the turn. It led to a small car park for dog walkers, bird watchers and anyone who enjoyed the nearby forest walks.

"Park over there and get out of the car."

Barnaby did as he was told.

When the driver's door had closed, Harvey got out and ordered Barnaby to the front of the car.

"Lock it, you can't trust anyone around here."

Barnaby locked the car with the key fob.

"Right, walk." Harvey motioned to a footpath that led into the forest. "Give me the keys."

"Now come on, this–"

Harvey made eye contact with him, and Barnaby handed him the keys. Unspoken words.

They walked for fifteen minutes, to a spot where the trees grew thick, and the undergrowth was full. The footpath faded to nothing and merged with the forest floor. Harvey spun the man around several times; Barnaby had to hold onto a tree when he stopped to steady himself.

"Belt."

"Belt?"

"Off."

"This is an outrage," said Barnaby as he slid the leather belt from the loops.

"Yeah, yeah. Socks."

"My socks?"

"Are you going to repeat everything I say, Mr Brayethwait? Because it's going to make what's left of your life very miserable if you do."

Barnaby slipped his expensive shoes off and pulled his socks off, offering them to Harvey.

"Throw them over there," Harvey nodded toward to the ground to his left.

"Okay, now we are ready to talk, but before we start, I think it's only fair that you know a little about me," began Harvey. "Why don't you sit down?"

"I'm just fine sta-"

"Sit down."

Barnaby sat with his back against the tree.

Harvey took the belt and wrapped it around the tree and Barnaby's neck. He made a new hole with his knife to make sure it was tight.

"That's not necessary."

"No, you're right, it's not. I am a very dangerous man, Mr Brayethwait. I have done things that would horrify you, give you nightmares. Do you understand? I've been doing these things since I was twelve years old, and I've got a knack for getting secrets out of people."

Barnaby's eyes were wide with fear. His hands were on the belt, easing the pressure on his throat, but he couldn't possibly reach the buckle, which was on the far side of the tree. A damp patch appeared on the tan pants Barnaby wore. Harvey looked down at it, then back up to Barnaby.

"That doesn't worry me, they all do that."

Barnaby began to cry.

Harvey let him cry. He would talk soon.

"It's gone too far. I can't stop them," sobbed Barnaby.

Harvey didn't reply.

"It wasn't meant to be like this, they were only supposed to offer-"

"Sex, Mr Brayethwait? They were only supposed to offer sex?"

Barnaby nodded, his eyes were shut tight; he sniffed a run of snot falling from his face.

"Have you, Mr Brayethwait?"

He looked up at Harvey.

"Have I?"

"Yes, Mr Brayethwait. Have you?"

"No, no, I would never–"

"Is that right? So you just go to the farm and what?"

"I *funded* some of it. That's all."

"So you haven't even had sex with the girls? Come on," Harvey reasoned, "a divorced man, high-pressure job. Surely a man–"

"*Okay okay*, I had sex with one girl. But *that's* all."

"Tell me, Mr Brayethwait, why did you choose *her*?"

Barnaby looked confused.

"Surely there were many girls to choose from, and you could have had any one of them, you funded it right?"

"Part funded, there were three of us."

"Right, so, why *her*?"

"I don't know, she was pretty. She was quiet with nice eyes and a nice body, why do men choose *any* girls?"

"All different reasons, Mr Brayethwait. Trust me, it takes all sorts. Was she young?"

"Younger than me," he replied stonily.

"Younger than *you*? How old *are* you, Mr Brayethwait?"

"I'm fifty-three."

"And how old *is* younger than you? Forties? Thirties? Twenties?" Harvey paused and watched Barnaby's face crumple. "Younger?" Barnaby nodded. His face was screwed up in a tight grimace. "*Eighteen?*" asked Harvey.

The sobs became audible then, spittle burst from Barnaby's mouth, and he began to pant; he struggled against the restraint around his neck.

"Younger still?"

Barnaby didn't respond, he just sobbed.

"Mr Brayethwait, was this girl younger than sixteen?"

Barnaby was crying uncontrollably, he nodded.

"Say it, say it loud and clear. You'll feel better. They all do. Confession is a glorious thing."

"She was..." Barnaby paused. "Fourteen or fifteen."

"And how do you know? Was it because she was developed, Mr Brayethwait? Is that it?"

"Yes, yes," he burst, "she was mature, she was just *young*."

"I understand, Mr Brayethwait. She was still petite and small. Did it make you feel like a big man? Is that it?"

"I didn't hurt her, I wasn't violent with her."

"Okay, so you treated her well? Did you stroke her hair? Did you caress her skin? Did you wish that she could be yours? Tell me, Brayethwait, what was her name?"

Barnaby spoke softly as if he was remembering it all, "Her name was Anastasia. She was lovely. Perfect in every way."

"How many times, Mr Brayethwait?"

He looked up. His eyes begged for understanding and empathy. "A few."

"I have one more question for you, and then all of this will be over."

Barnaby knew it was coming and broke once more. But when the words came, they hit him as hard as ever.

"Is Anastasia still alive?"

Barnaby wrenched at the belt. "*Let me go*, get me out of here, you can't *do* this."

"Tell me, Barnaby."

"No, no she's not. I did it. I killed her. Is that what you want to hear?""

"How?"

Barnaby settled, defeated. "Gently," he said softly.

"Gently?"

Barnaby looked up at Harvey, and stared him in the eyes. "I smothered her face, I suffocated her."

"While you were raping her?"

Barnaby nodded.

"Say it, Barnaby."

Barnaby hesitated then gave a deep sigh. "I suffocated her, while I was raping her."

"Thank you, Mr Brayethwait."

Barnaby kept his head down, his face was a mess of snot and tears.

"Mr Brayethwait?"

He looked up.

"Tell me where I can find Mr Cartwright."

"The farm," he snivelled.

"Thank you. And what is his role in all of this?"

"He brings the girls in from Eastern Europe. He has contacts. I paid for the farm, he brings the girls and-"

"And?"

"Jamie brings the clients."

"Like Oscar Shaw?"

Barnaby nodded.

"Jamie?"

"Jamie Creasey."

"Where does he find these clients?"

"She."

Harvey didn't reply.

"Jamie is a *she,*" said Barnaby.

Melody was sat in the passenger seat of the VW Transporter, Denver Cox was driving, and Reg Tenant was in the back manning the surveillance equipment. He had LUCY up on one of the screens and monitored Harvey's chips.

They were parked on the side of the road and had just watched Harvey follow the BMW into the car park on foot.

Reg watched as the chip on the motorcycle and the three on Harvey's person split.

"Harvey Stone down to three chips," he confirmed.

Two minutes later, the blue BMW pulled out of the car park and drove past them into the oncoming traffic.

"No point hiding, let's go," said Melody.

Denver pulled into the traffic then turned into the entrance to the car park. He reversed back onto the road, eliciting angry blasts of commuters' horns. Denver ignored them and joined the traffic. They could just make out the bright blue BMW in the distance.

"Be my eyes, Reg," said Denver.

"On it."

The morning traffic made for a slow chase, and by the time they pulled into the car park in the forest, the BMW was parked up and locked. Harvey and Barnaby Brayethwait were nowhere to be seen.

"According to LUCY, they're on foot moving fast through the trees in that direction," Reg indicated west and returned his attention back to the screens.

"Okay, you two stay here, I'll go alone," said Melody. She checked the clip in her Sig and holstered it.

"You wearing a vest?" asked Denver.

"Of course, but Harvey won't shoot me. If you see him, get me on the comms. Reg, I'm walking west, guide me when I need it. Otherwise let's keep radio silent, I don't want chatter while I'm listening for them."

She stepped out of the van and shut the door behind her, pulling her short jacket over her weapon.

"Okay, you're looking at about a mile. He's stopped

moving. Keep in that general direction, I'll steer you in," said Reg over the radio. She clicked twice on the ear-piece and ran through the forest as fast as she could. The track veered off south-west by an old oak tree. There was a wooden bench seat, presumably for walkers to rest. The trees were spread out at first, a mixture of beech and oak and some birch trees. But before long, the density of the trees thickened and the clumps of bushes between the tree trunks grew wilder and denser, which made travelling difficult.

"Eleven o'clock, Mills."

She tapped twice on the ear-piece and adjusted.

"You're two hundred yards out, Mills," said Reg quietly. "Hold on, Stone is on the move. Repeat, Stone is on the move. He's heading in a south-east direction, coming underneath you back to the car park, he must have seen us. His phone chip hasn't moved. He's left his phone behind."

"Reg, Denver, are you carrying?"

"We're both carrying," said Reg.

"Good, don't let him get away."

"You want us to *shoot* him?" asked Denver incredulously.

"Not if you can help it, but if you must."

"That's like poking a sleeping lion, Mills."

"Just don't let him leave. Okay, I have visual on Barnaby."

Melody walked into the copse of trees and found Barnaby tied to a tree. He'd soiled himself and looked up pleadingly at Melody.

Melody kept her weapon aimed at him.

She saw Harvey's phone on the floor and bent to pick it up. It was unlocked and had the audio recorder app open. She pressed play. Barnaby hung his head in deep shame. She zip-tied his wrists and released the belt, then walked him out barefoot without saying a word.

There was some commotion on the radio.

"Come in, boys. What's happening out there?"

"Erm, we have Stone. Hurry back, Mills." She picked up the pace and forced Barnaby Brayethwait to walk painfully across the forest floor through nettles and thorns. His comments on the discomfort were met with zero compassion.

"Okay, update, so we *don't* have Stone. Come on, Mills, he's getting away," called Reg over the radio. In the distance, she heard the BMW start and its engine rev loudly. Then she heard the whine of car's reverse gear and the crunch of tires skidding on loose gravel. She burst through the trees in time to see Harvey pull a J-turn around Denver who had tried trying to block his escape in the van. The BMW narrowly ducked around it with just inches to spare.

Reg saw Melody approach with Brayethwait and opened the back door ready to pull him in. She shoved Brayethwait into the van and dove in after shouting to Denver, "Go, go, go."

Denver didn't need telling twice, he found first and slammed the accelerator down. The rear-wheel-drive van reacted instantly, and they shot forwards. He over-steered onto the main road with a long screech then straightened up and homed in on Harvey in the BMW ahead. Melody reached up and closed the rear door, and zip tied Brayethwait's ankles before climbing over into the front passenger seat.

6

THE FARM

HARVEY HIT STOP ON THE RECORDING ON THE AUDIO APP and placed the phone on the ground away from Barnaby in a clear patch of dirt so that Melody would find it easily.

He checked Barnaby's restraint and turned to face him.

"Six months ago, you'd be a dead man. Consider yourself very lucky."

He turned and ran south, then cut east back to the car park from a different direction. He burst out of the trees and used the key fob to unlock the BMW. The indicators flashed once, and he heard the door locks pop open.

Fifty yards down from the BMW was the VW Transporter. Reg had the side window open, and his Sig hung out in the open air, pointed directly at Harvey.

"Don't move, Harvey. I'm really sorry, but I can't let you go."

Harvey froze and lifted his hands. He turned to face the van, he was expecting some sort of effort to stop him.

"Nice try, Reg." He lowered his hands and opened the car door.

"I mean it, Stone. Don't *make* me do this," he called from the window.

"Do it, Reg. You couldn't hit a double-decker bus from that distance." Harvey climbed into the car and fired up the engine. He heard the gunshot and, as predicted, Reg fired high.

Harvey selected reverse and gunned the throttle, spinning the wheel to drive backwards out of the car park. If he drove forwards, Reg might have a better chance of getting lucky and hitting him through the windscreen, but the odds were slim.

He wound the engine up and reversed towards the rear of the van, just as Denver reversed to block his attempt at getting past. Harvey was expecting that too. Denver was a far better driver than Reg was a marksman. Harvey span the wheel, braked, and slid the stick into first gear, performing a textbook J-turn and narrowly missing the rear of the van. He straightened up and kept the throttle down as he joined the road. The rear end of the car slid out nicely as the BMW's computer system controlled the power to the wheels. He shifted into second, third, then fourth and settled in for the drive.

The van emerged from the car park in Harvey's rearview mirror. He knew that Reg would have LUCY open and they'd find him regardless of how fast he drove, so he took it easy on the winding lanes, maintaining his distance and keeping the van in view.

He felt along the seams of his jacket as drove and reached deep inside the pockets. Finally, he found a small lump in the stitching by the zip. He reached around and pulled his knife from its sheave on his belt, then cut through the thick leather with the sharp blade. He tossed the small chip out the window, then put his foot down.

Harvey took the turn into Pudding Lane in less than

thirty minutes and began a slow crawl to the entrance of the driveway. A game plan was formulating in his head, but there were so many variables and unknowns, it was too early to execute. He had always been able to run scenarios through his head, possible outcomes, pros and cons; it was one of Julios' influences. Sometimes though, the old Harvey shone through, and he went with his gut.

He was four hundred yards from the farm entrance when a silver BMW X5 nosed out of the driveway. He flashed his lights to let the car out. A female hand waved a thanks through the passenger window, and Harvey could just make out long, curly hair through the rear window.

He slowed and let the car pull out, then hung back to allow the women to get out of sight, then pulled into the farm. He drove up the bumpy track and stopped outside the old wooden barn.

The small area where drivers obviously parked outside the old, run-down barn was still devoid of cars. Barnaby had reverse parked his car outside the Epping Labour Party office, so Harvey reverse parked too. People generally notice small breaks in habits, thought Harvey. The parking area was around thirty metres by thirty metres with a faint track that led off behind the buildings.

Harvey climbed out of the car. The buildings were in an L-shape. The front building was small and derelict with two floors, and the second building was more of a barn come warehouse. It had a small door on the right and two large sliding doors to the left for farm machinery and trucks to reverse up to.

Walking to the smaller door, he studied the keys on Barnaby's bunch and selected the correct key first time. He pushed the door open with a gentle squeak and stepped into the dim light.

He noticed the smell first of all. It was an air freshener,

sandalwood. Harvey thought it odd that somebody would choose to freshen the smell of what was essentially an old barn. He quietly closed the door behind him and let his eyes adjust to the shadowed room. Throughout the old building, jagged light infiltrated the many gaps in the structure's joints. The barn's contents were clear, but the details were vague in the semi-darkness.

He stood still and listened, but heard nothing. There was a small flashlight in his jacket pocket, a two-cell torch that was small and light, and he barely even noticed it was there. Harvey flashed the light around.

Sitting just inside the large sliding doors was a small digger. It was a rental and had the number of the rental firm on the side of the boom fixed to the bucket.

Along the back wall was a series of old stables. The low stable doors had been replaced with much newer and larger ones that offered no view into the six pens. Each was locked with a padlocked hasp and staple, and a deadbolt into the floor.

A long steel beam ran through the centre of the building from end to end. It looked like it may have been used to shift hay, or even cattle or horse feed, from one end of the room to the other using the small rope block and tackle that hung from a trolley fixed to the beam.

In the space beside the sliding doors, there was a pile of blue plastic sheets. They weren't the cheap plastic type sold in hardware stores, they were thick and heavy. Beside them, on the floor, a hose was curled up and fixed to the single tap on the wall.

To Harvey's right was a spacious area with some old couches. Somebody had made an effort with the arrangement, but the couches had deteriorated in the old barn.

A door to the left of the couches was left open. Inside, Harvey found a kitchen. Its cleanliness in such a building was impressive. It was like somebody had recently put a lot of effort into making it presentable, perhaps somebody who was charging clients a lot of money for the services they rendered there. Harvey thought of Donny and his fine taste. He wondered if, while the barn was not spic and span and likely never would be, he had some sort of say in the cleaning of the kitchen.

A smaller door led off the kitchen. Harvey pushed it wide open. The room was pitch dark inside. His torchlight fell onto screens that had been fixed to the wall. Each one had a glowing LED. indicating the on button, and the hum of a computer indicating that it was running.

He reached up and turned the first screen on, the red light turned to green, and the display lit up. It showed a dreary, monochrome image of the BMW out front. He turned the second screen on. A small room with what looked to be an iron-framed bed in the centre of the space. At the edge of the room was a bucket and a plastic container, presumably for water. On the opposite wall, Harvey saw a bench with items hanging on the wall. The camera angle was poor so he couldn't see exactly what they were, but he guessed there would be rope and chains plus various sharp implements and other sick devices.

The third screen was the same. The fourth screen was a little different. It showed the monochrome image of a similar small room with a similar bed in the centre. This room had two buckets by the wall, no bench with torture devices and three girls sitting and lying on the bed.

One girl sat with knees drawn up underneath her. Another laid with her back to the camera, and the third stood up and began pacing the room. Harvey turned all the screens on. Of the six stables, only two had girls in; stables three and four had three girls in each. Three of the stables looked as if they had been made ready for guests. The last looked the same as the ones that had the girls in, but was for the time being, devoid of life. Harvey guessed why.

He turned the screens off and walked back to the main barn. He touched one of the six locked doors with the flat of his palm. There was life behind the solid wooden panel. But that particular life was not Harvey's concern. Donny was Harvey's concern. Once he'd dealt with Donny, then he could help free the girls. If he tried to free them now, he risked losing Donny for good.

As he walked to the small door, Harvey heard a car arriving; its tyres crunched on the dirt. The BMW X5 had just pulled into the entrance and was slowly making its way up the track. Harvey looked around the room, then up. He ran and jumped, grabbed hold of the steel beam that ran along the ceiling and pulled himself up. He balanced on it and walked to the end, where it met the wooden truss of the roof. Making his way across the network of joists, he stopped above the kitchen in the darkness of the ceiling space.

He heard a heavy car door close outside, and the door to the barn swung open. The person wasn't hiding their arrival. The sound of heels on the poured concrete floor stopped.

"Barney?"

There was no answer.

Harvey watched as the woman stepped slowly over to stables three and four and pulled firmly on the padlocks to make sure they were locked. She was tall for a woman, and the heels made her taller. Her thick mass of loose curly hair bounced as she walked. She wore a two-piece suit with a frilly blouse that protruded from the collar of her jacket. Her skirt was shorter than knee length, and she looked to be in good shape. Harvey judged her to be late thirties.

"Barney?" she called again, like she was calling her dog.

Again, there was no answer.

She stepped into the kitchen out of sight. Harvey tracked

her footsteps through the gypsum ceiling, he imagined her walking to the control room. She wouldn't start with screen one and work across. Instead, she would start with screens four and five to check the girls were there and alone. Then she would turn on the others; nothing, no sign of him. She wouldn't find Barnaby Brayethwait anywhere.

Harvey tracked her as she walked back out of the kitchen and stood in the centre of the open barn. She pulled her phone from her handbag and dialled a number. Harvey noticed that there were just three clicks; phone app, recent calls and then the number. It was too far for him to see if it display a name.

"Hey, is Barney with you?" Harvey heard the one-sided conversation. "No, his car is outside but he's nowhere to be seen. I thought he'd be having his way with one of them, but the girls are all in three and four, and the other stables are empty." She moved to the doorway and stood looking out at Barnaby's BMW. "No, I'm going to feed them, then get back to work. What time will you be here?" There was a pause while the other person talked, then, "Okay, and Bruno? I'm not doing the buckets again." Another pause. "Okay, I'll lock up, maybe he's just left his car here. I'll be back tonight around seven-ish, can you ask Bruno to muck the stables out and hose the girls down? I have a client coming at eight and I want them clean. When are the new girls arriving? Tomorrow? What time? Okay, I'll make their room up. I'll see you tonight."

She stepped into the kitchen and Harvey heard the sound of boiling water. Cupboards opened and closed, and crockery was moved about. Five minutes later, she emerged again with a tray of three bowls of what looked like porridge. She set them down outside room five, opened the door and set the tray inside without a word. She locked the door and did the same procedure for room four before returning to the kitchen, retrieving her handbag and walking to the door.

She stepped out and pulled the door closed after her. Harvey heard the lock click into place and the rattle of her keys as she stepped away to her car.

Harvey walked across the wooden beams and stepped on the steel joist. He walked along then hung down and dropped to the floor. He unlocked the door and opened it a fraction. It was clear, so he stepped out and locked the door behind him.

Moving quickly, he unlocked the BMW, climbed in and started the engine, then tore along the bumpy driveway. He turned right out of the farm entrance, the opposite direction to where he'd seen both Donny and the woman head to. He drove directly to Epping, through the town centre and passed where he'd parked his bike earlier that day.

With no sign of the VW, he pulled the BMW into the car park of a nearby supermarket and walked casually back to his bike. He was careful to avoid direct exposure to the cameras that were sporadically fixed to the street lights in the car park.

Harvey unlocked the back box, removed his helmet, and within thirty seconds was joining the light traffic on the road out of Epping. It felt good to be riding again; Harvey wasn't a fan of cars, they felt too claustrophobic.

He ran through the scenarios in his head. Ideally, he would find Donny in the farm on his own. But the mention of Bruno, who Harvey assumed was the man driving the Toyota SUV behind Donny the previous day, gave Harvey doubts. If Bruno was to be mucking out the stables and be around when the client was there, presumably he was not intellectually involved in the operation. He possibly provided some level of security. That was Donny's style. He would give the impression of wealth by having a minder to disguise his cowardliness.

In an ideal situation, Harvey would have surveillance hardware from the team, but he couldn't exactly call them up and ask to borrow some binoculars and a Diemaco sniper rifle. Hopefully, the capture of Brayethwait had stroked Carver's temper a little.

Harvey decided to overshoot the farm and spent the remaining daylight off-roading. He worked his way through the fields to come upon the farm from behind. If he could find somewhere to stash his bike, he could then sit and watch the play. Patience.

Julios, his mentor, had drilled into him the importance of patience and planning. Harvey would need to know routines, schedules and habits. He would need to identify the players, work out the pecking order and find a way to isolate Donny. It would be easy to pull up alongside Donny's Mercedes at traffic lights and shoot him through the glass, but suffering would be minimal. Harvey was not an unkind person. But, in his mind, the only way to really pay penance for an evil was to suffer in a similar fashion; it brought a certain balance to the world.

The house where Harvey and Donny had grown up and where Harvey had boiled Sergio alive wasn't far from the farm, perhaps fifteen minutes. Harvey was very familiar with the area and knew a way into the farmer's fields behind the barn.

His BMW motorcycle was as capable off-road as it was on tarmac, and soon it was spitting mud from the back end as Harvey wound his way along the edges of the surrounding fields. A thick copse of trees stood behind the farm. It was perhaps five hundred yards from the buildings, which meant that Harvey would have to crawl five hundred yards.

Harvey pulled his bike into the trees and removed his

helmet. His view of the barn was far from perfect, he would definitely need to get closer. The fence that ran behind the barn spread far across the fields. All along the underside, there were thick wild grasses, nettles, and occasional black-berry bushes.

Laying on his front, Harvey made his way along the fence and pulled his weight with subtle movements of his feet and forearms. Each movement gained four to six inches. It took him two hours to reach the barn, but when he did, he was confident that nobody from any direction had spotted him. He parted the grass slightly in front of him, which gave a clear view of the barn's front side from thirty metres away. Even if somebody walked up to the fence, he would remain unseen under the growth that grew beneath it.

At six-forty-five, the BMW X5 turned into the farm's entrance and headed slowly up the track. Jamie climbed out. She was unlocking the single door of the barn when the Toyota SUV turned in and made its way up the drive in a far more reckless manner. It bounced in the potholes and large dust cloud formed in its wake.

Jamie didn't wait for the other car to arrive, she disap-peared inside. The Toyota skidded to a halt in the dirt in front Harvey. The dust cloud followed it a few seconds after, so Harvey closed his eyes to protect them and covered his face with his shirt.

By the time the dust had cleared, the driver was already out of the car and opening the door to the barn. Harvey caught a glimpse of the man. He was big, very big. That didn't frighten Harvey, not much did, it just meant that if he came to blows with the big man, Harvey's approach would need to be tailored to suit. Large muscular men tended to have beef protecting their organs, so a throat attack was often more suitable. This was slightly more tricky as a forceful blow to the man's throat could kill him. Harvey didn't necessarily need to kill him. Unless, of course, he deserved it. Time would tell. For the time being, the man was just a barrier between Harvey and Donny. It made the challenge more exciting.

Another thirty minutes passed when Donny's gleaming Mercedes came into view. Donny took the bumpy track slowly, manoeuvring the large saloon around potholes. He came to a stop in the spot nearest the door. The engine was cut and the door opened, and Harvey saw his foster brother for the first time in six months.

7

SNEAKY PEEKY

SIX MONTHS BEFORE, WHEN HARVEY HAD FOUND AND tortured Sergio, he had given up Donny's name. Donny had, at the time, been in the Maldives pretending to be dead following an attempt on his life by a rival gang, the Thomsons.

It had been the perfect timing for John Cartwright to stage his own son's death, which effectively took the Cartwright family out of the running for the diamond heist that was being planned.

The heist attempt had not gone ahead. The Cartwrights had lost their weapons, and John Cartwright had gone missing. Donny returned a month later to find his best friend, Sergio, killed, his father missing, and his father's house a crime scene. The northern job was carried out by an unknown, and the family business was in ruin.

With what little capital he had left, Donny had to make a new start on his own. Without the financial backing of his father, and the support of his father's resources, it had been a struggle, but he'd met with an old friend, Barney, who had, in turn, introduced him to Jamie.

Donny still had a giant target on his back in the criminal society. So he'd hired some protection in the form of Bruno, a former bare-fist knuckle fighter in East London's underground scene.

Bruno wasn't just a bodyguard, he was Donny's conduit to the outside world. Before Donny went anywhere, Bruno would arrive up to thirty minutes beforehand to make sure the route was safe, and the location was secure. If it wasn't, Donny would not move.

Bruno stood nearly six-foot eight and out reached most men in the ring. He weighed a formidable one hundred and forty kilos, most of which was solid bulk. His one flaw was that he was slow by boxing standards. His last few fights had been with smaller and faster opponents, and he'd taken many blows to the head. He'd still won, but his head had taken a beating. He often landed only one or two punches, but that was all that had been needed.

His career had left him slow in the head. He had some money, enough to live on, but it wouldn't provide a lavish lifestyle by any means. Donny had seen him and stepped in, offering the huge man a way out.

Bruno's slow mental ability did not affect his instincts or his eye for danger. After nearly two decades on the underground scene in East London and South London, he'd had his fair share of vicious attacks, from bottles, knives and guns. Men who had lost money waited in the car park of the pub or in a dark back alley. He had a sense for danger and an immensely powerful body.

Donny was a business genius, but a shallow coward. The two were well suited.

Donny stepped into the barn. His aftershave overpowered the sandalwood air freshener that neutralised the odour of fifty years of horses and four months of Eastern European girls using buckets for toilets.

"Ah, you're here," said Jamie from the couch area of the barn. She had her laptop open and was finishing an email. Donny ignored her.

"Bruno, where are we?" he said.

"Just finished mucking out, boss. Need to hose them down, though yeah?" Bruno said with a grin.

"That's right, Bruno, the client will be here in half an hour, let's get them cleaned up." Bruno smiled and unlocked stable four.

"Knock knock, ladies, it's bath time," he said in his slow, baritone, lazy grumble.

Donny turned to Jamie, "Who's the new client?"

"Some hotshot lawyer from the city, has a place out in Ongar. Said he heard about this place from a client of his."

"Who? Are we running checks on these people? We're not letting *any* old Tom, Dick and Harry in are we?"

"We are certainly *not* letting in any old Tom, Dick or Harry, Donny. He's been vetted, paid up front, cash. He said if it's what he expects, then he'll make it regular."

Right then, Bruno came walking out of the stables with three girls in tow. He held a brown leather strap that was fixed to the first girl's neck, which in turn was attached to the next girl, and that one to the third. They could easily unfasten the collars, but they knew better than to try. They had all been stripped of their clothing and walked behind him, ashamed and embarrassed, to the far wall where Bruno took the leather strap off.

Donny stood and watched as Bruno handed each of them a bar of soap. Then he uncoiled the hose from the reel on the wall and tested the pressure.

"Are we ready, ladies?" he said.

The first girl was dark haired, with dark features but pale white skin. She was physically flawless. She had no fat on her body whatsoever. Her chest was small but pert, and her legs were slender. She was just sixteen years old, the youngest of the girls. She was also tough. She stared hard at Bruno as he turned the hose on her.

"Get washing, come on, you need to wash those bits and bobs, for Uncle Bruno and his massive-"

"Bruno, come on mate, he'll be here soon, no time for fun and games. *You* can have a go later, once the client has gone," said Donny.

"You can't keep letting him do that, he'll ruin them," whispered Jamie in a harsh tone.

"Oh come on, Jamie, he don't get *many* pleasures anymore, look at him. He leads a simple life does our Bruno, it keeps him going. Look how happy he is."

"Hey, Bruno,"

Bruno turned, "Boss?"

"How happy are you right now?"

Bruno gave a low, clumsy laugh, followed by a large intake of air into his huge lungs.

"See what I mean? Leave him alone, he'd never *hurt* them."

"I think Barney has been visiting a little too often too. Honestly, how you expect the girls to be in any decent condition by the time you guys have all had your way, I do not know."

"*Oy*," said Donny holding his hands up defensively but smiling. "*I* haven't been tainting the goods, I don't need to, thank you very much. Anyway, where is Barney? Haven't heard from him all day, it's not like him."

"I saw his car earlier, and I messaged him, but haven't had a reply."

"Let me know if you *do* hear from him though, I'd like to get the budget sorted out. I'm thinking we should expand the operation."

"*Expand?*" said Jamie. "Into *where?*"

"A new place, Jamie. I'm thinking we should keep the location moving. Always into a bigger place. See if we can get six months rent on the next place, and double the number of rooms, then do that again after six months-"

"I thought this operation was only for a year, so we could all make a quick few quid. It's not exactly a *career* for me, Donny. I can barely sleep at night."

"Jamie, it's not my ideal career either, I can assure you, but let's face it. We can do this *and* earn well, or we could go work in an office, for peanuts."

"The money isn't *that* good, Donny. I mean, it's good, but it's not going to make us millionaires. We keep having to buy new girls."

"Bigger picture, Jamie girl. I want to bring more girls in, up the quota. Right now we've got six rooms, two of them are bedrooms, the others are for the clients. So we can have four clients come in at any one time. I want to put the girls out to farm first. Have them earn their cost. So clients who don't want to go for the premier package as it were, can still get their rocks off. Once the girl has earned her cost back, she can move to the next room, ready to be offered to the premier clients. Then it's the big bucks

"Its a *barn*, Donny. It *stinks*."

"I'm putting the prices up too," said Donny, ignoring her. "Premier is seventy-five thousand. The pikey package will be a grand for an hour. She'll only need ten pikeys, and then we can offer her to a premier client, Jamie. Come on, you don't look impressed."

"Did you hear what I said?" Jamie put her hands on her on her hips and furrowed her brow as she looked at him, "It's a *barn*, it *stinks*."

"Well, so what, we have to start somewhere, Jamie. Look at Bill Gates, he started in his parent's basement or something. We can turn it into some kind of wild west theme, that way we wouldn't have to do a lot to it. Maybe have a bar as well, punters would *love* that."

"He was making *computers*, Donny. You're offering prostitution services to wealthy gentlemen who get their kicks from killing the girls. The idea behind prostitution is one that has stood the test of time. Girls sell their bodies for sex, over and over. It's a reusable commodity. Your whole methodology sucks. Are you going to implement some kind of just in time inventory management? How do you plan on keeping a steady flow of girls coming into the country?"

"Jamie, you bring the clients, I'll bring the girls. I told you. I have a good contact, and he hasn't let us down yet has he?"

"The last batch were nearly dead when they got here, how the bloody hell is he getting them in the country?"

"Jamie, do I ask you how you get your clients?"

"Yes, as a matter of fact, you did about ten minutes ago."

"Okay, well do I criticise your methodology?"

"What's to criticise?"

"Did you hear about Oscar Shaw?"

"Oscar Shaw?"

"The very famous stage actor who was in here about three weeks ago, you remember him?"

"Yes, of course I remember him, he tipped very well, had two girls didn't he?"

"He bloody died. Police found him in his dressing room didn't they? Naked with some actress. They'd snorted ant killer or something, anyway, police found a flash drive with a video of him here with the two girls."

"No way."

"Yep, it was in the papers."

"Can they trace it back to here?"

"No, impossible. He called a burner."

"Boss, I'm done, they're all clean," called Bruno from the other side of the barn.

"Righto, Bruno," Donny replied, then lowered his voice again. "Just relax, Jamie. Trust me, I've been on the wrong side of the law my entire life, it's in my blood. And I'm not stopping until my bank account says I don't have to work another day in my life." He left her with a serious stare and turned to Bruno.

"Good work, Bruno, my son. Good work." The six girls were lined up and connected by their necks again with the leather straps. "Right ladies, let's see those smiles then. Who's going to be the lucky one tonight then, eh? Which one of you beautiful girls is going to meet the man of your dreams tonight? Because you do know the rules don't you?"

They looked at him, scared but defiant.

"Whoever gets picked, gets to go home, you get to say goodbye to your little family here. So, go on, when the client arrives. Make him welcome. Won't you?"

Bruno stood behind him grinning. Donny noticed him. "Okay girls, new approach, whoever doesn't get picked tonight will have to take this fella on, and I wouldn't want to be on the receiving end of that, I can tell you."

Jamie grinned at his joke from the other side of the barn and caught Donny's eye. He's a sick bastard, she thought.

The sound of tires of the dirt outside silenced the room. "Bruno," said Donny, and with a slight movement of his head, Bruno was out of the barn and standing guard at the door.

Jamie slipped out beside him, "Ah, Mr Narakimo, how are you, sir? Did you find us okay?"

"Stone is down to one chip," said Reg from the back of the van. "He must have tossed it back there."

"It's okay, I figure we know where he's going," said Melody.

"How about us? We can't drive around with *this* guy. Can't we drop him off at a police station or something?" Reg was forced to sit close to his bench with Brayethwait laid on the floor behind him.

Melody called Frank, he picked up on the first ring.

"Carver."

"Sir, we have one IC-1 male in custody, name of Barnaby Brayethwait. We have an audio confession pertaining to the rape and murder of a minor and also highlights Cartwright and one other, a Jamie Creasey."

"Good work, well done. What's the plan now?"

"Observe and report, sir."

"Excellent, keep me informed at all times. Where's Stone?"

"We believe he is heading to the farm, sir."

"Is he going to blow this whole thing apart?"

"No, sir. I do not think he is. He had the opportunity to finish Mr Brayethwait and chose to leave him for me to find. I think he knew that it would buy him time."

"What's the plan, Mills? Once Stone goes in you'll need to go live."

"Sir, we need to get Brayethwait to a police station so he can be formally charged under the correct procedure. If we drive him around in the van all day, his lawyer will kick up a fuss."

"Okay, where's the nearest station? Where are you now?"

"We're heading our of Epping, we are in pursuit of Stone, however, Tenant has him on screen so we can keep an eye on him. I suggest we take Mr Brayethwait to Chigwell, sir. We can be back on Stones trail pretty quickly after that."

"Okay, Mills. I'll call ahead so they're expecting you. I look forward to your next report."

"Yes, sir."

"Oh, and Mills?"

"Sir?"

"Work *with* Stone. Watch him. If he let this Brayethwait guy live, maybe he'll leave us some more crumbs. Hole up and observe."

"Yes, sir."

Carver disconnected.

"Chigwell nick, Denver. Let's get rid of this guy."

They took the drive out to Chigwell and found the police station quiet. A desk sergeant greeted Melody with a half-smile. The paperwork was ready for her to sign, and Barnaby Brayethwait was led off to start a new life behind bars, his head hung low in shame.

Melody climbed back into the van. "Sitrep, Reg?"

"Okay, so Harvey drove straight past the farm, into Loughton, then turned around and went straight back. He is currently inside the barn."

"He's inside?"

"That's what LUCY says."

"He's crazy."

"Find us a spot we can hole up in. Somewhere close by."

"Got it, I found the perfect place. Denver, let's go," said Reg, rearranging his chair now that Brayethwait had been removed. "Mills, let's pick up some snacks or something. Last time we holed up, all we had was petrol station food."

"Shame you don't have a stove back there, you could cook for us as well."

"You wouldn't want my cooking, Melody, but I do make a mean cheese sandwich."

"A cheese sandwich? That's literally just cheese, bread and butter."

"Yep."

"And what is it that *you* do differently to the rest of the planet that makes *your* particular cheese sandwich worthy of the *mean* award?"

"Get me to a store, and I'll show you."

"Denver, you heard the man, let's find a mini-mart or something, then hole up. Reg, how's our man doing?"

"He's still inside, I need eyes on the building though."

"It'll be too risky in the daylight, I can do a recce when the sun goes down, maybe fix a camera to watch the door."

"Ah, we'll see," said Reg, "I may be able to help there."

The three drove past the entrance to the farm and Melody looked up the track as they went by.

"There's two cars there. The blue BMW and an SUV. He's not alone."

Denver took the next right. It was a small dead end that led into some fields, but the foliage around the lane offered plenty of cover for the van. It was an ideal spot away from prying eyes.

"What's he doing? You don't think he-"

"No, I don't think he's in there tearing the place up. I think that SUV belongs to our friend, Jamie Creasey, and Stone is taking notes, and waiting for his brother to arrive."

"Foster brother," Reg corrected.

"Okay, so maybe I can cut through this field in front when it's dark, and plant a few bugs on the outside. If we can capture audio, we can build up the case from there."

"Why don't we just put a camera on the front door? Then we can see people going in and out."

"That's fine, Reg. Why don't I sneak carefully through the field and plant the audio bugs while you take a stroll up the front drive and install a camera? They might even make you a cup of tea if you ask nicely."

"Nah, I prefer to work at my desk, you know me. However, have I introduced you both to Sneaky-Peeky?"

Denver turned in his seat, "What are you talking about, Reg?"

"Sneaky-Peeky, Denver." Reg lifted a modified radio

controlled challenger tank with over-sized tracks and a camera in the place of the turret. "See? It peeks, while it sneaks." The lifelike scale model of the tank was two feet long and weighed just fifteen kilos.

"No," said Melody, "too risky."

"Ah, come on. You haven't even seen the best bit. Reg reached down into one of his sports bags. "I'm still working on this, but I think it'll save millions of lives."

"Millions of lives?"

"Well, yours at least, Melody, but we have to start some-where." He pulled out an elasticated olive-green scrim net that fit perfectly over the tank without getting caught on the over-sized tracks. It had a hole in exactly the right place for the turret cam. "See, we can just stuff a load of grass under this, and drive *slowly*. Slowly is the key to stealth remember. If we go tear-assing up the drive with this, it'll be spotted a mile off, but sneaking isn't about going fast. Sneaking is about being sneaky isn't it?" He looked proud of himself. "Hey? Come on, it's *brilliant* and you know it."

Reg slid the open top of the VW, and let the chill into the van. He stuck a magnetic antenna on the roof and extended it as high as its telescopic sections would allow, then connected the cable to a VHF port on his computer's network card. He opened the back door, pulled up some grass from behind the van and began tucking it under the netting.

"Sneaky-Peeky reporting for action, ma'am," said Reg, mimicking a soldier.

Melody smiled at Denver who was shaking his head and holding back a grin, "At ease, soldier."

The silver BMW SUV drove past the dead end lane where they were parked, heading away from the farm.

"That was the car in the farm, the SUV. I'm sure of it," said Melody.

"So Harvey is in there alone?" asked Denver, "Shall we go get him?"

"No, Frank just wants us to observe. Harvey will do one of two things. He'll be on her tail, if that *is* indeed Jamie Creasey, or he'll hightail it out of there and wait for Donny Cartwright. My money's on the latter."

Melody cracked the window.

"How are we going to know if we can't see the driveway?" asked Reg.

"Shh," said Denver, "that's the sound of a BMW M3." They heard the distant engine in the quiet countryside.

"How do you know that?" asked Reg disbelievingly.

"Shh," Denver hushed him again, "unmistakable. Definitely an M3." The engine noise faded away.

"Looks like he's gone to find Donny. Reg, how's he doing?" asked Melody.

Reg glanced up at the screen from where he stood at the rear of the van tinkering with the tank. "Yeah, he's on the move."

"Reg, how close does the tank need to be?"

"I'd say two or three hundred yards, but one hundred would be better. It has a seventy to three hundred mil lens and will capture 4K video at thirty frames per second."

"Okay, get that tank into position, I don't know how long this window will be."

"Roger that."

8

OLD FACES

HARVEY LAY STILL BEHIND THE FENCE. HE FLEXED HIS FEET and fingers to keep the circulation going. The cold ground made his clothes damp and uncomfortable, but he'd waited for longer in far worse conditions. He'd once stood in a park near Stratford in the freezing cold snow for an entire day, waiting for a known sex offender who had been released from prison. Harvey had watched him over several weeks, and found no pattern at all in his timings, but he took the same route whenever he walked his dog. Harvey had bit the bullet and waited from the dark morning to the dark evening before the man finally came along. Harvey had done what he needed to do, and then took the man's confused dog to a vets.

A large Bentley Continental turned its broad, elegant nose into the long driveway and drove slowly along the track. Its large wheels managed the potholes with ease and eventually, it took a wide circle to park alongside Donny's Mercedes.

The driver got out. He was a short Japanese man whose horizontal frown matched his unsmiling mouth. He walked to the passenger door and opened it like it was second nature, offering the passenger a curt and discreet bow as he climbed out.

"Thank you, Hiroki-San." The driver returned to the vehicle and climbed back into the sleek car.

The barn's single door opened, and the large man stepped out. He was a man who looked like he was always ready for a fight. He looked questioningly at the small Japanese man who stood in front of him. Jamie Creasey slipped out of the door and beside Bruno, "Ah, Mr Narakimo, how are you, sir? Did you find us okay?" She had the ability to please people, she was a saleswoman.

"Come in, please," she continued, "we have the girls ready for you. Have you travelled far?"

"I have a modest house in Ongar," said the Japanese man, "I use it when I am in London. I do very much enjoy the English countryside." His English was very clear with no sign of his Japanese heritage.

Jamie and the Japanese man stepped inside. Bruno glanced around the area, which was growing dark, and pulled the door closed behind him.

The driver remained in the car. This was an issue for Harvey. He needed to get close, but couldn't arouse suspicion. Making a mental note of the number plate, he worked his way along the fence until he was out of sight of the cars behind the barn. He swiftly jumped over the wooden fence, being careful not to disturb the grass that grew naturally underneath the wooden cross beams; that would leave a sure sign that someone had been there.

Harvey stepped up to the rear of the barn. There were no windows, no doors and no gaps in any of the wooden panels that clad the old building. There were also no visible cameras. The security had been tight on the inside and at the front, but anyone could stand at the rear.

He put his ear to the wall and listened. Nothing. Harvey

stopped and thought. The Japanese man would likely want the most privacy, so stable one would probably be his room of choice. Harvey judged the distance and listened to the wall. Nothing. The thick wood absorbed any sound from inside. Harvey stepped back to look up at the roof. Perhaps there was a way in, but he couldn't recall seeing a skylight. His foot sank into soft soil, much softer than the ground he had been stood on.

He glanced around him and noticed the patch of ground where he stood had all been freshly dug. The darker patch of earth was roughly eight feet by four feet and not symmetrical or neat. It was the hole of somebody who had used a small rental digger but hadn't quite mastered the skills.

At least one more body would be buried tonight, thought Harvey, then crept back to the fence and jumped over. He dropped to the ground and crawled slowly back to his original position. No change in the scenery.

Harvey planned.

The Japanese man would leave. Harvey imagined it would be Bruno who dug the hole. Donny wouldn't carry out manual labour himself. Harvey's plan all depended on who left the farm first. Jamie or Donny.

Harvey laid beneath the fence that ran behind the farm. He had a clear view of the long driveway, the side of the barn where the doors were, and the fence that ran fifty metres adjacent to the track, connecting the road to where Harvey laid.

Movement caught his eye. Dusk was fading to darkness and shadows had a habit of playing tricks on the mind. He watched the area of wasteland between the track and the fence. Someone or something was moving towards the barn, but he couldn't quite place the position. Each time he looked, the area looked slightly different. Something was out of place.

He checked his own surroundings. Maybe the team were

closing in. That would only leave Melody. The other two clowns wouldn't stand a chance of not getting caught.

He glanced back at the waste ground. Something moved. Just fractionally. Harvey locked onto it. It was small and covered in grass, which had made it hard to spot. He moved along the fence until he was in line with it, then jumped over into the waste ground. He had seen the view of the cameras and was sure that camera one didn't reach any further than the cars. He crawled over to the movement and came up behind it. It was a radio-controlled tank.

Reg.

He smiled.

Harvey crawled up behind the tank. He heard the soft whir of the tiny motors that operated the turret. He pulled back and returned to his spot. Occasionally he glanced at the tank. It sat completely camouflaged in the long grass.

Less than two hours after the Japanese man had entered the building, the door opened once more, and he stepped out into the cold night. The lights from inside lit the ground around him. He had on a business suit. No tie. A knee-length Kashmir coat and a long silk scarf. Donny and Jamie stepped outside with him.

"Well, I hope the experience lived up to your expectations, Mr Narakimo."

The man paused and looked around into the darkness. "Yes, Mr Cartwright, it most certainly did. It was a..." he sought the word, "thrilling experience."

"I am pleased, and did Anna accommodate your needs?" asked Jamie.

"What if I said no, Ms Creasey? How would you punish her?" he offered a cruel grin.

"Well, I was just seeking feedback for future experiences, Mr Narakimo," said Jamie, sheepishly defending her statement.

"I can assure you both that I am more than capable of providing adequate feedback." He smiled. "I like the set up here. It could be more elegant, but I think the primitive decor rather matches the offering."

"Thank you, Mr Narakimo. We're actually planning on expanding, perhaps we can offer you a return visit?"

The little Japanese man laughed. "Please do not offer me a coupon. It's not a coffee shop."

Donny smiled warmly. "No, Mr Narakimo, but for valued clients such as yourself, we could perhaps improve the value you receive. As we get to know you more, we can tailor the experience. You may find your tastes develop each time."

"Ah, Mr Cartwright, you have a head for business. I shall return. Do you mind if I bring guests?"

"Of course not, Mr Narakimo. But please do give us advance warning. We'd like to ensure that each of our clients has choice and, as you can imagine, we do like to make sure that our operation remains a safe and discreet place for us all."

Mr Narakimo nodded, "Mr Cartwright. Miss Creasey. Good night."

The Japanese man made his way to his car. His driver must have been listening as the driver's door opened the moment Mr Narakimo said the words *good night*.

The Bentley moved off and made its way back along the long, bumpy driveway. A satisfied customer sat inside.

"Bruno, let's go, we have a hole to dig," Donny called and clapped his hands.

Harvey remembered Donny's whiny voice from his childhood. Donny would use the same tone to call his father, John, when Harvey had done something wrong. "Dad, Harvey broke the window." Or "Dad, Harvey won't do what I tell him to." John hadn't risen to the whines of his spoiled son and had often turned the information on Donny himself. A life of crime had hardened John to grasses or informers, and he had tried his best to ensure that his own son didn't become one.

Donny hadn't grown up to become a grass or informer. He had learned the lessons, but he still had the traits of a man who led a very wealthy childhood and had never gone without.

Harvey had never gone without either, not in monetary terms, John had seen to that. But he had lost his sister at a young age, because of Donny, which made his foster brother the last man on Harvey's list. His time was growing near.

Harvey had also never fully been told about his parents. John had always said that he and his sister had been found in John's bar. Harvey had been in a hamper with a blanket. His elder sister, Hannah, sat beside him.

John's wife, Barb, had wanted to adopt them, having only one child of their own. And so Harvey and Hannah's discovery had not been reported to the authorities. Instead, they had been driven back to the family house where, over time, the life of money and crime had become a way of life for Harvey. For Hannah, it had become the end. The desires of John's closest men had proved too much for the teenager.

Harvey had vowed for her vengeance, and was closing in on his final target.

The sound of the mini-digger's diesel engine starting up broke Harvey's thoughts. He checked his surroundings. The tank was still sat in the long grass. Jamie had gone back inside, her car was on the driveway. Donny was stood outside and the two large sliding doors screeched open allowing Harvey a clear view of the inside. The bright lights that hung in the eaves of the barn shone unnaturally onto the ground outside. Harvey checked the tank. He couldn't see it, but he knew it was there. From where Donny stood, it would just look like a clump of long grass. It was, however, moving slowly backwards, Reg had obviously thought the same thing about the lights.

Sitting in the small seat of the digger was the massive frame of Bruno. He looked ridiculous, like he was using a toy. He pushed two levers, and the tracks began to roll forwards out the barn with a loud grumble that reverberated through the ground to where Harvey sat. Bruno steered the heavy digger out of the barn and turned right around the corner to the rear of the barn, where Harvey had stood an hour before and found the soft ground.

The diesel engine revved angrily and filled the night. The two lights fixed to the top of the cab swung above Harvey as the machine passed by where he lay. The diggers engine was turned off, and Harvey heard Bruno starting the job with a shovel.

Donny picked up one of the plastic sheets from the floor and dragged it open. He positioned it directly in front of the doors in Harvey's direct sight, and in front of the tank that sat patiently amongst the long grass.

Once the plastic sheet was pulled out, Donny stood in the open and breathed in the fresh air. Jamie joined him.

"It's so peaceful out here," she said, alerting him to her presence.

Donny gave a soft snort of irritation and looked back to her.

"Yes. It is. I can almost hear the sound of fifty pound notes landing in our bank accounts."

"Do you ever think about anything else but money?"

Donny stepped forward and leaned on the fence, directly above where Harvey was laying. Harvey stayed perfectly still, he was tucked under the growth of grass and thorns.

"Yeah, I do," he said sullenly. "Often."

"What goes through that mind of yours? What eats you?"

"Ah, Jamie. We've done a good job so far of keeping our

relationship purely business-like. Let's not get too familiar, eh?"

"What are you hiding, Cartwright?"

Donny took a breath and held it, "We all have our skeletons, Jamie. Where do you keep yours?"

"I'd love a skeleton or two, Donny, but that would mean letting people in. Something I was never good at."

"You don't need to let people in to have skeletons. Sometimes they arrive uninvited. Then destroy everything you have."

"Sounds painful."

"It is." Donny sounded subdued. "My father had it all, you know that?"

"Yeah, everyone knew John Cartwright."

"He started with one bar and built up an empire. Pretty soon any bar in East London that was worth having either belonged to, or owed money to, the Cartwrights. That's where I learned about business, from my old man. I stood to inherit all of it. I would have been set up for life, Jamie." He laughed. "What a joke, eh? Now look at me, I'm in the bloody prostitution business. My old man would do his nut if he could see me now. He hated hookers."

"What actually happened to him?"

Donny looked across at her suspiciously, the question had been quick. "No-one knows, Jamie."

"Yeah, yeah. I know that's what your lot say when someone's in hiding."

"God's truth. The Thomsons had me marked, they were-"

"The rival family, yeah, that was all public knowledge."

"Right, well, they put a hit out on me. Nearly worked as well." Donny reached up and touched the scar tissue on one side of his face. "I survived though, and my dad saw it as a good time for me to pretend to be dead. So I was sent off for a few months. By the time I got back, it was all gone. The bars, the banks, the men, the houses. And my dad. There was nothing left."

"You haven't heard from him?"

"I doubt I ever will to be honest. He's either dead or working on his tan. He won't be back either way."

"But you're his *son*. How *could* he just forget about *you*?"

"Listen, Jamie, when you're up to your eyeballs in the life we lead, the moral compass gets a bit off balance. Know what I mean?"

Jamie nodded.

"We did things that none of us were proud of. Things that we never spoke about again. We never really stopped to consider what would happen if the truth were to come out in the open. Or if the people we cared about found out about those terrible things. We didn't even consider the consequences of those things ourselves, let alone how they would impact the people around us." Donny took a lung-full of air and noisily blew it out through his nose. "My old man has long gone. I don't deserve anything he could offer anyway."

"That's a shocking thing to say, Donny." Jamie almost had a caring tone to her voice.

"Don't *pity* me, Jamie. What doesn't kill us makes us stronger. I'm coming back, Jamie. I'm making my *own* money." He turned to face her; half his face was lit by the bright white lights from the barn, his scar was hidden in shadow. "And *that* is what will make my old man *proud* of me, more than anything else in the world."

The lazy starter motor of the mini-digger broke the night's silence, and they both turned to see Bruno's massive bulk inside the small digger's windowless cab. The arm of the machine dug greedily into the soil.

The two walked away, and Harvey breathed out. Donny had been his foster brother for as long as he could remember, but he'd never ever witnessed any kind of emotion from him other than hate, spite and anger. The feelings had been mutual. Harvey was the lost kid who inadvertently stole his father's attention when they were young. If Donny had scored a goal at football practice, John would have missed it because he was tying Harvey's shoe. If there was extra meat at dinner, Harvey would have it because, although he was younger, he was already bigger and needed more food.

When they'd grown older, Harvey was still treated differently. Harvey didn't cry, whine, or complain to John. He dealt with his own issues, while Donny wondered why nobody heard his cries. It was by Donny's own design that he was kept at arm's length.

Then the final straw had been when Donny and Sergio had raped Hannah with Jack. Hannah had brutally killed herself. John had known what happened. Not much got passed the old man. But he protected both Donny and Sergio from Harvey. He needed Sergio to run the business and Donny was his own flesh and blood. But the incident had caused John's wife, Barb, to leave him, and John hadn't fully trusted Donny ever since, choosing to nurture a relationship with Harvey instead. Someone more befitting his trust and fatherhood.

Harvey understood now. Donny's perspective had slotted things into place. Donny would still die a slow and awful death, but he had unwittingly answered some of Harvey's questions.

He checked the tank, it was still sitting there. As far as the investigation was going, Melody and the boys would have indisputable evidence of Mr Narakimo going in and Mr Narakimo leaving, and then a hole being dug for a body. The evidence against Mr Narakimo would not be irrefutable, but Donny, Jamie and Bruno would be in a very bright spotlight, and there was always DNA to fall back on.

When the digger was turned off, Harvey watched Bruno

stumble in the darkness, then shuffle into the barn. He disappeared and re-emerged carrying the young girl's dead body.
She was dark haired, very petite and her limbs hung loosely
from Bruno's strong arms. Bruno laid her on the plastic sheet
and folded one side across her. Then he rolled her until the
lump in the sheet was unidentifiable, and folded both ends of
the roll inward, securing them with gaffer tape. He placed the
tape back on the shelf, then hoisted the long blue parcel onto
his shoulder.

Harvey was sickened. He had seen death for most of his
life. He'd even played the role of death and dealt it out with
his own two hands. But that had been to people who had, in
Harvey's mind, deserved pain and suffering. The girls that the
brute was dumping in the ground deserved nothing of the
sort. Harvey would seek their retribution. He would make
sure the sins against them were paid in full.

Harvey heard the dull thump as the body hit the ground.
Then the scraping of soil on the shovel began as Bruno began
to fill the hole. He worked slowly in the dark. His only light
was the two harsh lamps from atop the cab of the digger.

Donny and Jamie had disappeared inside the barn.

When he was done, Bruno once again broke the silence of
the night and drove the digger back to the barn. He switched
off the engine and silence resumed.

"Boss, all done," he announced.

"Great, let's go home, Bruno."

"But, boss..."

"Sorry, buddy. You can have some fun with them tomorrow," said Donny in a quiet voice, so that Jamie wouldn't hear.
Bruno's face lit up. He'd become like a simpleton and Donny
was manipulating him. That was Donny's style. "Lock those
sliding doors up, Bruno."

"Jamie, see you tomorrow," Donny called.

She came out from the kitchen. "You're leaving?"

"Well yeah, what else is there to do?"

"Maybe wait for me," she said.

"Ah Jamie, you're a big girl."

Bruno pulled the two large sliding doors closed. The space outside was plunged back into the darkness of the countryside, and Harvey heard the metallic sound of locks. Then the single door opened, and Donny and Bruno walked out. They both got into their separate cars. Donny didn't wait for Bruno, he started his long and bumpy trip in his Mercedes, while Bruno pulled in behind him. The Toyota SUV handled the bumps just fine, although Harvey saw that the driver's side was considerably lower.

Harvey watched as Donny and Bruno drove away. He needed Donny alone, but Bruno was always there by his side.

The single door opened, and Jamie stepped out. She clicked the button on her key fob; the BMW's indicators flashed once, the locks popped open, and the interior light slowly came on. She was about to lock the door when she noticed the light was still on, so she stepped back inside. Harvey vaulted the fence. He ran quietly to the car, opened the passenger door and slipped his watch under the passenger seat. He saw the lights turn off, so shut the door quietly and crouched down low, slowly moving back into the darkness of the waste ground. He turned and motioned to the tank, tapping his wrist with two fingers.

Jamie climbed into the car, and the interior light dimmed. She tapped out a message on her phone, then dropped it into the centre console, selected drive, and accelerated away.

Harvey took a walk around the back of the barn again to see where Bruno had buried the new body. He wondered if he was making new holes, or just dumping fresh bodies into the same pit. He found the fresh dirt. Bruno had dug a fresh hole right next to the first one. The job wasn't neat, but Harvey expected that was to do with Bruno's inexperience with the digger.

Harvey thought about digging a hole for Bruno, an extra large one. He might even make him dig his own hole, then bury him alive while the girls watched. The thought process was all part of Harvey's planning process. One thing was for sure, he would make sure the guy paid for his sins.

TIME

MELODY CARRIED SNEAKY-PEEKY TO THE ENTRANCE OF the driveway. She set it down in the grass to the left of the track. Reg immediately took control, and the tank began to trundle away towards the fence that ran adjacent to the driveway.

She headed back to the van unseen and walked around the rear to where Reg was sat with the large single rear door wide open. He sat on a modified office chair that had the casters removed so it wouldn't roll around on the wooden floor of the van.

In front of him were two screens and a laptop. The laptop showed the main interface of LUCY. In the centre of the screen was a satellite image of Harvey's tracking chips. It was a mess. His watch chip was in a field behind the barn. His motorcycle chip was nearly a kilometre away several fields behind his watch. His phone showed as being exactly where Melody stood, which it was, holding the audio confession of Barnaby Brayethwait. The chip from Harvey's leather jacket was on the side of a country lane in a ditch around five miles away.

The main screen showed a high-resolution live feed of Sneaky-Peeky's turret camera. It was moving extremely slowly through long grass beside the fence.

"That's a pretty clear image," said Melody.

"I modified a DSLR. Sneaky-Peeky has two built-in SD cards and a 70-300mm telescopic lens. It's capable of recording 4K resolution onto the SD cards and providing live feed at full HD, which I can record from this end. It gives us a little bit of resilience against the loss of Sneaky-Peeky itself." Reg grinned.

Melody sighed, "Okay, Reg, I know you want to tell us more, go on."

"Thought you'd never ask," he said. His smile was nearly as wide as his face, "Not only can it operate for close to five hours, due to the configuration of batteries," he added, "but, I tore some of your surveillance hardware apart, and integrated the technology with the DSLR." He continued to grin and waited for Melody to ask more.

"Well?" she said, "What does all of that mean to simple folk like Denver and I?"

"I stole your NV goggles and stuck them on the turret with the camera. It's fascinating inside those things. I'll take a closer look when I get a chance."

"You stole my night vision goggles?" asked Melody.

"Only one pair, you still have another pair," he replied defending his actions. "Besides, now Sneaky-Peeky has night vision, and you can sit in the nice warm van." He turned to her, he was beaming. "Sometimes, Melody, you can almost taste my genius."

"Eyes on the road, genius," she said, nodding at the screen, "or you'll be tasting the sweet scent of grass because it will be you that has to run down there to ask for your toy back."

"Oh, how she mocks. Denver, are you hearing this?"

"I am," said Denver, who was watching the road in front for any sign of traffic that might be slowing for the turn into the farm. "But I wish I wasn't."

"Do you both honestly think that I would send Sneaky-Peeky, my beloved creation, into the wilderness without a map?"

Melody raised her eyebrows.

"Sneaky-Peeky has built-in GPS. I just plug in the coordinates and hit go, and it'll go straight there. I can enter sets of coordinates if I want it to follow a particular route, or if we have the CAD file of a building, it can read the directions from LUCY."

"Can we send it to Burger King then?" said Denver.

Melody smiled at the dynamics of the two, "Where exactly are you sending it?"

"Right here where the two fences meet." Reg pointed at the spot on the screen. "From there we'll have an uninterrupted view of the front of the barn."

"We need eyes on the driveway. I want a heads up when cars come in or out."

"I only have one Sneaky-Peeky, Melody, but soon I shall have a fleet." He said the last words with a sinister undertone and winked at her.

"Looks like I am going for a walk after all," she said, and left to prepare herself. She slid open the side door of the van and pulled her kit bag from under the passenger seat. She took an extra clip for her Sig, a small Maglite, and fitted her ear-piece before pulling on a tight, black woollen hat. She grabbed her jacket from the front seat and pulled it over her black Norwegian army sweater, then stuffed her NV goggles into a small pack.

She turned away from the van and took a few steps. She tapped the ear-piece button, "Comms check."

Her voice rang clear from the speaker next to Reg's laptop, "Received, repeat," he replied.

"Loud and clear," she said. "Okay boys have fun without me."

"Wait one," said Reg. He found Melody's tracker chips in the directory on the left of LUCY's interface, and ticked the box next to her name, so all of her chips showed up on the satellite image.

"Good to go, three chips live. Phone, watch and purse," said Reg. "You're up on LUCY."

"Okay, I'll just be across the road there with eyes on the driveway. I won't get close as the tank-"

"Sneaky-Peeky," Reg corrected her.

"Sneaky-Peeky has the front covered."

She slipped away, and the two men watched her cross the road and duck into the thick tangle of bushes that lined the far side.

The light was fading as she made her way along the fence that ran behind the barn. She pictured the eyes on the barn. The tank was at the front looking directly at the doors, and Harvey was behind the fence to the side of the doors. He would have a clear view inside if the large doors opened. And Melody was tucked behind staring at the side of the barn with no windows or doors. The sky grew dark until she could no longer make out the shape of the building. She moved closer, and found a spot hidden from view. She could see the driveway clearly but not the doors. Reg would need to handle that.

Three cars arrived within thirty minutes of one another. The BMW SUV arrived first with a female driver. That was Jamie Creasey. She reported it over the comms and Reg confirmed. Then two more cars arrived; another SUV and a large, black Mercedes saloon.

"Confirm, the second car is Donald Cartwright," said Reg.

"Who's in the first car?" Melody asked.

"Hold on, I'm just on Sneaky's night vision. I don't have a name for him, but holy crap he's big."

"Say again."

"I said, the man is big. He just had to turn sideways to walk through the door."

For the next thirty minutes, Melody sat in the dark. It was frustrating not being able to see the doors, but she knew that nothing was happening there either. The action was on the inside.

Another car turned into the driveway.

"It's busy tonight."

"Can you see the plate?" asked Reg.

Melody read the plate number to him as the car drove past her. She heard it come to a stop and two doors open and close.

"The car belongs to one Narakimo. Unmarried. Owner of several Japanese export firms, he has offices in Threadneedle Street, EC2. He's of Japanese descent and has a value of... wow." Reg went quiet.

"What's wrong, Reg?" asked Melody.

"I'm counting zeros."

"Okay, so he's rich."

"That's a fair statement."

She heard the door bang closed.

"You think he's a client or a partner?" she asked the two men.

"Client," said Denver.

Melody was intrigued. Denver rarely voiced an opinion, he was the strong and silent type.

"What makes you say that, Cox?"

"How much is he worth?"

"Many, many zeros," replied Reg.

"Okay, so the guy's a successful businessman. Clearly, he has a head for the ins and outs of business."

"Right, where are you going with this?" said Melody quietly into the mic.

"Do you honestly think that a guy with that many zeros after his name would start a brothel? And would he start a brothel with a known criminal?"

"You're right, he's just a sick and twisted rich man," said Reg.

"So, if he's a client who wants sex, why come to a barn in the middle of nowhere? Why not have hookers sent to his plush apartment in the Docklands?" asked Denver.

"Because what he wants to do can't really be done in his plush apartment," said Melody. "Guys, I can't sit here while a girl dies in there."

"Melody, we're observing remember. Sit tight."

"No, Reg. How can I honestly live with myself knowing that I sat behind a barn when on the other side of this wall someone was being raped and murdered?"

"Reign it in, Mills. Come on, no emotions here, put them away," said Denver, the voice of reason.

"Cox, someone is going to die here tonight, she might be dying now."

"If we blow this and they get away then the girls who have already died did so for nothing. Come back to the van, Mills."

"Since when do you give the orders, Cox?"

"When you're out of control. Get back to the van and let's talk it out. If it makes sense, we'll call Frank, and he'll get us back up, but right now you need to get back to the van."

"Cox-"

"These comms are recorded right?" asked Denver.

"Yes, direct to file," replied Reg.

"So there's a direct order on file, Mills. We have all the authority, it's a closed loop, if one of us loses control, the others can take action. Come on now. Come back to the van, let's talk it out."

"But the cars-"

"I have all the information on Mr Narakimo we need, Melody. I also have a file auto-populating on Bruno Mason. He's the big guy. Sneaky's in place to get video, they have to get rid of the body through one of those doors and Sneaky will record it."

"If another girl-"

"If another girl dies, Mills, we'll deal with it. Get it together," Denver cut in. "If we compromise the operation and they get away, more girls will die."

There was a silence.

"Mills, do I have to call it in?"

Mills fell back into the field and made her way along the fence to the road. She climbed through the hedgerow and walked casually across the dark, empty lane into the dead end turnout where the van was parked two hundred yards down. Reg slid the side door open as she approached.

"I'm not happy about this one bit," she said, slinging her small pack into the back of the van. She began to remove her hat and coat while Denver and Reg waited for her to calm down.

"No-one is asking you to be happy about it, Melody," said Denver. "Listen, I'm sorry I had to do that, but we're not equipped to go kicking doors in and making a bust. There's three guys in there and one woman, any one of them could be carrying."

"Harvey's there too."

"Yeah, we know Harvey's there, but our objective is to observe. Harvey is no longer on the team."

"Yes he is. He wouldn't have left Brayethwait alive if he was off the team. You heard the confession. You know Stone."

"What makes you think Stone would back you up?" asked

Denver. "He's a villain deep down. Besides he doesn't care about the girls or Creasey. He's after Cartwright. That's where his head's at."

"He would have backed me up," replied Melody, reaching around to retie her hair back, "he's one of us now."

Denver turned away shaking his head, then looked back at her. "You really think so?"

"Of course," she snapped, "we *have* to think that. We *have* to believe he's on our side, or what else have we got? Nothing is what. We can't alienate him."

The two men fell silent. Then Denver spoke, "Take the comms off."

Melody pulled her ear-piece out, and Reg paused the recording. He nodded at Denver.

"If you want to *believe* that Stone is on our side, then we need *him* to *know* that we're on his side. Otherwise, he'll just think we're out to bring him in, and that Frank will put him away."

"How do we get a message to him? I have his phone, and he doesn't have comms."

"Sneaky-Peeky to the rescue," said Reg cheerfully from the back. "Talking of Sneaky-Peeky, the camera just went dark. Small glitch, we're back up, not sure what that was."

Melody and Denver were watching Reg work the tank's camera. He focused on the large Bentley and zoomed in on the dark windows. "There seems to be someone still inside the Bentley."

"Mr Narakimo's driver maybe?" said Denver.

"Possibly, hold on, it's moving. Hey, *I'm* not doing that." The camera shifted from the car to the double doors.

"What *was* that?" asked Denver.

"Stone," said Melody, with triumph in her voice. "Does that thing have a speaker we can talk to him through?"

"Um, no. But I'll make a note, and Sneaky-Peeky *Two* will have."

They waited for it to move again, or for Harvey to show himself on the camera. But enough time passed for them to realise he was gone again.

"We have action," said Denver.

They watched as Mr Narakimo stepped out of the barn, followed by Jamie Creasey and Donny Cartwright. They stood and chatted for a while. The body language suggested that Mr Narakimo held the power, while Creasey and Cartwright tried to please him. Reg tracked him as he walked to his car, and the driver emerged and opened the passenger door before returning to the driver's side. The night vision picked up the heat from the engine, glowing brightly in contrast to the surroundings.

The Bentley pulled away and then the whole scene turned white.

"Turn the NV off," said Melody.

Reg switched the NV off and turned the turret back to the barn. The double doors were open, spilling light out onto the forecourt. The big man, Bruno Mason, sat at the controls of a digger, filling the cage that served as a cab. Two bright lights fixed to the top of the cage came on, and the digger's exhaust began to emit clouds of black diesel smoke.

The digger rolled out of the barn and turned right around the back of the building. Its two bright lights bounced through the darkness and then out of sight.

Cartwright stood by the fence at the edge of the screen and looked out into the night. He was joined by Creasey. They talked inexpressively for a while until the big man returned from the rear of the barn and entered the double doors. He dragged a blue plastic sheet to the open space at the front and then disappeared. He reappeared with the limp, dead body of a young female.

Melody gave a gasp.

"Easy, Mills, we knew what we were getting into here. Reg, is this recording?"

Reg double checked. "Yep, we have video evidence of three suspects disposing of a dead body, and one more who has just left the building, who I am sure will have left some kind of DNA on the victim's body."

The three were transfixed as the huge man causally wrapped the body in the tarp, and tied it off with gaffer tape. He worked quickly and efficiently then easily hoisted the body up onto his shoulder and walked past Creasey and Cartwright, back behind the barn.

Before long, the lights of the digger bounced back along the narrow walkway between the rear fence and the building, then turned left into the barn. The engine was killed, which kicked out a chuff of black smoke, and the lights were switched off.

Five minutes later, the two men left the woman there in separate cars, and Jamie Creasey prepared to leave.

The headlights of the two cars flashed past the top of the turnout where the team were parked.

"Okay I have Cartwright's phone via GPS. I can follow him home," said Reg.

"Good, track his every move, but we also need eyes on Jamie. She's the low hanging fruit," replied Melody.

The lights of the BMW flashed on, then faded as the interior brightened. Jamie fumbled with the barn door then disappeared inside once more.

"What's that?" said Reg. "See that shape?"

They saw the passenger door of the BMW open, and Harvey's silhouette place something under the seat. He closed the door again, and the shape faded away as the barn door reopened and Jamie came out. She locked the barn then climbed into the car. There was a short pause, and she pulled away. Sneaky-Peeky was left staring at the barn.

"NV," said Melody.

Reg switched the night vision back on.

Harvey stepped into view and walked to the building. He glanced back at the camera then slipped around the back to where the digger had been working.

"Shall I follow him?" asked Reg.

"No, wait a minute. What's he doing?"

Five minutes passed. Then ten. Harvey did not re-emerge. "Okay, bring Sneaky back, Reg," instructed Melody.

Sneaky's extract was much faster than the journey in. It was pitch dark, and there was little chance of anybody returning, so Reg set the tank to return to their GPS coordinates. He watched the screen as it made its way along the country lane and turned to drive toward the van. As it drew near, he opened the rear door and stepped out.

Immediately his arm was twisted behind his back. His body was turned, and his face was pushed hard onto the wooden floor of the van. He went down with an audible grunt.

"Hands on the roof."

Melody and Denver began to turn, "Hands on the roof, I won't ask again."

"Stone, did you enjoy the show?" asked Melody.

"Hands on the roof or I break his arm." Denver and Melody slowly raised their hands to the roof of the van. Harvey increased the pressure on Reg's arm.

"Ow, ow, you're hurting me, ow," whined Reg.

Melody and Denver pushed their palms flat against the roof.

"Okay, do I have your attention?"

"Undivided," replied Melody.

"Good, I'll do you a deal."

"A deal, Harvey? Why don't you just come back and we finish this together? It's not too late. I can talk to Frank."

"I'll talk to Frank myself."

"Frank won't be in the mood to talk to you if you hurt one of us, Stone. Come on."

"I'll give you the girl, you give me Donny's location."

"You know where she is?"

"Roughly. You know where he is?"

"Roughly. Why should we trust you?"

"Because you're still alive."

"And Brayethwait?"

"A gift."

"A gift?"

"From me to you. To get some brownie points."

"We can all do well out of this if we do it right, Harvey."

"Doing well is not my objective, Melody."

"What's your objective?"

"Same as it's always been."

"Hannah?"

Harvey didn't reply.

"Reg, are you okay there?"

Reg's face was held against the floor, "I've been better."

"Are we recording?" asked Melody.

"No, we turned it off." Reg spat dust from the floor away from his mouth.

"Okay, Harvey, but it's bigger than this. We want you on the team. I'm talking long term. Once all this is over, we can go back to normal. You're an asset. I can help get you back in. We all can."

"I need to do this-"

"I know, you've spent your life chasing this, I can't imagine how that must feel to be so close. But hang in there. Trust us."

"Trust you?"

"I know that's hard, honestly. But we can do this, and all get what we want." Melody paused. "How about you let Reg go, he's a bit fragile."

Harvey didn't reply.

"Okay, have it your way. How about we give you Donny, but you help us take this down. Rescue the girls, nail Creasey and the Jap, and plug the hole where the girls are leaking in from?"

"I don't need you to give me Donny."

"No, but you need us to give you freedom. Frank will have you put away for this. For everything you've ever done. You know he has that power. But I know he doesn't want to. I know he wants you on the team, just like we do. Right boys?"

The boys each grunted affirmatively.

"I'm taking Donny anyway, we can talk after."

"You don't know where he is."

"He's on the screen."

"What about Creasey?"

"What about her?"

"You give us Creasey, we give you Donny, right? It's what you said."

"You find her when the time's right."

The pressure on Reg's arm relaxed, and he slumped to the floor rubbing his shoulder.

"What's that supposed to mean?"

Harvey didn't reply.

BEWARE OF THE BEAST

ONCE HARVEY HAD RETRIEVED HIS MOTORBIKE FROM THE copse of trees in the field, he found the road in the dark and made his way to Loughton where he'd seen Donny on the screen. Donny was inside the small apartment block that Harvey had seen him and the Bruno enter the previous day. So he parked his bike in a back street, stashed his helmet in the back box and continued on foot.

It was gone midnight, midweek, so the roads were quiet. Cabs owned the roads in the early hours, carrying drunk businessmen returning from the city after a night with clients or colleagues, who would probably need to steal into their house to avoid waking their spouses. Then tomorrow they'd do the same thing. It was an endless cycle.

Harvey liked his freedom, he preferred not to become tangled with the same woman; too many questions, too much emotion. Once you spend your life being trained to dispel emotions and set them aside, it's hard to call them back. He'd tried to have a girlfriend several times, but each time they got heavy, and Harvey would back off. They'd complain he was too cold and didn't show affection. He'd treat them right, more than right. Show them a good time, nice restaurants, walks in the wild, he even took one on a weekend break to the Lake District, so they could walk in the mountains and see the beautiful lakes. But they always wanted more than what Harvey had to offer.

The apartment block was situated on a corner where a small side road ran onto the high street. It was four storeys tall and had a high wall around the property. To the rear, trees poked above the brick wall, and Harvey imagined there was a lawn, flowers and some kind of outdoor seating for the occupants to enjoy on rare sunny days. If the property had been in France or Spain, there'd be a pool.

The entrance to the underground car park was at the front of the building to the right of the main doors. Harvey walked past the building once, and found the cameras without breaking stride. By the time he had walked two hundred yards further and turned back, he had a plan.

A building like that rarely employs a full-time security guard. The cameras probably weren't manned, but were there for the footage to be called upon should an incident occur, which in Harvey's mind was ridiculous. He could get into the building, rob an apartment, or worse, and then leave. Sure the cameras might have his face on camera, but he'd be long gone.

A lesson he had learned from Julois was that acting like you were doing nothing wrong drew less attention than trying not to be seen. So he walked casually up to the top of the entrance ramp and strolled in around the barrier. There were no whistles, no alarm and no security guard calling after him. He walked to the bottom, turned into the car park and looked around for Donny's black Mercedes.

It was parked next to the silver Toyota SUV that the big

guy had been driving. Donny must have him living there full time, which meant he was either waiting for something to happen to him, or just plain paranoid. Donny had never been paranoid before, he was overly confident if anything. He had a brilliant mind for business but no backbone.

Six months previous, after Harvey had been asked to take out the son of the rival Thomson family, they had retaliated by putting a hit on Donny. John Cartwright had seen this coming and had Harvey shadow Donny. Harvey had managed to pull Donny out of a burning car and probably saved his life. He didn't do it for love, he didn't do it because he cared about his foster brother; he did it because that was what John had paid him to do. Harvey had often thought about watching him burn. It wasn't until after the event that Harvey discovered Donny was one of three men that had gang-raped his sister, Hannah. If he had known Donny had been involved, Harvey would have taken pleasure in watching him burn.

The Mercedes was parked in space thirty-five, the Toyota in thirty-four. On the wall behind each of the vehicles was a small sign with the apartment number the space belonged to. Harvey guessed this was to stop other residents using the wrong spaces. The sign behind the Mercedes and the Toyota read, Aptmt 204.

He strolled casually over to the glass door of the hallway. Two large elevators had their doors closed. The digital numbers were still. The building slept.

The door was locked, and had a small electronic card reader to one side; flashing a security card in front of the device would release the magnetic lock. Reg would have the door open in seconds. Reg would no doubt be able to hack into the building's security system, find the network where the doors were located and release the locks, maybe even control the lifts as well.

Harvey was not as technically gifted as Reg. Harvey had a much simpler approach to life that required minimal technology. Of the team, Harvey related to Denver more than Melody or Reg, but he was growing to like them all. They were all different, they'd led different lives, but he respected their skills.

Melody was fantastic at what she did, she had a great mind, was tough and could shoot better than any of them.

Denver had been a villain himself until the government put him into a program to nurture his skills in an environment more conducive to doing good. His proudest moment was having two police helicopters and more than a dozen police cars chase him across the country. The chase had made the news, and he had eventually outsmarted every police driver and both the pilots; he had got away.

Sadly, people with great technological minds like Reg had installed speed cameras, and Denver's image had been captured in a stolen Ferrari. He was arrested for the theft of over eight million pounds worth of high-end supercars and given the ultimatum to either join the rehabilitation program or go to prison for a very long time.

For Denver, the choice had been simple. He ended up being trained by the country's top drivers and pilots and taught how to use his skills to create a legitimate career. He'd been a real success story.

Harvey stepped around the walls of the car park until he found what he was looking for. The breaker box was locked, but the lock was just a plastic key insert and a weak metal barrel. Harvey ripped it open, and the catch on the inside fell to the ground by his feet. The building was designed for use by private residents, which meant that the public areas had to conform to British standards. One of the standards defining the safety and security of electricity circuits stated that each device or outlet in a public space must be labelled with the circuit number and identifier. Harvey found the circuit that matched the label on the card reader and flipped it off.

Another British standard that defined the fire evacuation protocols stated that, in the event of a power outage, all magnetic locks must release, allowing doors to open without hindrance. Presumably, so that people weren't trapped inside a burning building.

Harvey strolled back to the door and pushed it open.

He stepped inside and pushed the button to call the lift. He heard one of the lift's mechanisms clunk into life, the other remained dormant and in power save mode.

He rode the lift to the third floor, stepped out of the elevator and found apartment 304. It was likely that 204 was directly below, with both floor plans being identical, so Harvey had a good indication of the layout of the building. The apartment was to the right of the fire escape at the end of the hall.

A quick walk down the fire escape stairwell brought Harvey to the second floor, he opened the door a fraction and saw the front door of 204 at the end of the hallway. He half expected Donny to have the big guy sitting outside like a guard dog, but the hallway was apparently empty.

He slipped out onto the soft carpet. The hallway was nicely decorated with ornate patterns in the mouldings and coving. The lights were modern and the carpet was thick and expensive. It was the type used in hotels that are designed to withstand heavy foot traffic but remain aesthetically pleasing.

Harvey walked slowly and quietly along the hallway, the apartment door was fifty feet from the fire escape. Along the way, Harvey found service doors. A cupboard with cleaning implements had been left unlocked. Another door marked *Telephony*, was locked, and the last door marked *Electricity* was also locked. He reached the end of the hallway and stood in front of the door marked *204*.

He had several options, several plans, all of which were a risk. He ran through the scenarios in his head. Option one, set fire to the front door. The other residents might hear the alarm, leave and be safe, but Donny would burn. This was a drastic option and relinquished control to the ferocity of the fire. There were too many variables, plus collateral damage. Harvey preferred his victims to die deservedly where possible.

Option two, set the fire alarm off. When Donny came running out, Harvey would slip into the apartment and wait for him to return. This option also had flaws. Nobody listened to fire alarms, they went off accidentally too often. Also, he had a greater risk of being seen by other residents.

Option three. Ring the doorbell.

Reg climbed back into the van, leaving the rear door open. Melody came around and checked his arm for breaks.

"You'll be fine," she assured him. He winced as he pulled his sleeve back down and exaggerated his pain as he lifted his arm to the bench.

"Let's have a sitrep, Reg. Take your mind off your arm. Where are the players?"

He took the mouse and refreshed the screens.

"Okay, according to LUCY, Cartwright is two miles away in Loughton."

"That's his home, right?"

"I believe so, LUCY shows regular prolonged visits and there's no indication of him having a partner."

"Creasey?"

"We don't have her number yet."

"Stone?" she said hopefully.

"One mile away in Hainault. Travelling fast."

"That was quick, Denver, let's go."

Denver started the van, Melody picked up Sneaky-Peeky and placed it inside the vehicle. She closed the rear door, walked around and climbed back into the front passenger seat.

"Why are we tailing Harvey?" asked Denver.

"Well, we know Cartwright is at home sleeping. My guess is that Harvey won't go near him with Bruno anywhere nearby, so Stone is probably on the tail of Creasey. He said he knew her whereabouts, he'll lead us straight to her."

Denver put the van in gear and entered the chase.

They drove in silence. Denver concentrated on the road, speed cameras and efficient driving. Reg guided him with infrequent updates on Harvey's movements. Melody stared out of the window, deep in thought.

She tried to empathise with Harvey. He was throwing away his ticket to freedom, but would she do the same? How must it feel to have chased somebody your entire life and be so close to finding them? Harvey had lost his parents at an early age and had never found out the truth behind their deaths. He had witnessed the rape of his sister and waited twenty years before finally learning it was his foster brother. His foster dad had known all along which made it worse. Just one of those things would have broken most people. But all of them together? What damage does that do to somebody?

Melody had seen the remains of Sergio, the second man of the three had had gang-raped Hannah. Harvey had boiled him in an antique copper bath. She remembered the claw feet, and Sergio's clawed hands gripping the bath's rolled edge.

Harvey was a stone cold killer, but she saw something else in him. She saw the good. He was turning. He had left Brayethwait for Melody to find. A crumb. If he *was* after

Creasey would he leave *her* for the team too? It made sense. With Creasey out of the way, only Cartwright remained, which meant a far greater chance of getting him alone. But the team needed to plug the hole. They needed the source of the girls. Stopping Cartwright would only mean that the source would probably find a new conduit. It wouldn't be a solve, and subsequently, more girls would die.

They'd been on the road for forty minutes when Melody snapped out of her thoughts. She focused on her surroundings and saw the One Canada Square tower out of the passenger window.

"We're going to the Isle of Dogs?" she asked.

"We're just following Harvey," said Denver.

"Actually, yes we're going to the Docklands. He's outside a club there. Marco's, according to LUCY. You think Creasey is in there too? It'll be a hell of a place to have a showdown."

"I don't think he'll take her out in a bar, too many eyes. He's observing. Planning. Have you seen him work?"

"Harvey? Of course. He's a psychiatrist's dream."

"It was part of his training. He told me once when we were sparring. Patience, planning, and execution.

"You sparred with Harvey?" asked Reg incredulously.

"Yeah, a few times. He's good. He's-"

"A killer. He's a killer, Melody."

"He's a good fighter. He lets you attack him and watches your every move. It's like *he* knows what you're going to do before *you* do. It's the most frustrating thing. He knows that. He lets you get frustrated and studies your strongest side and your weakest moves. Then out of nowhere, he pounces."

"Like a wolf," said Reg.

"Like a lion, Reg. Patience. Planning. Execution. That's what he told me. His whole life is run by the same mantra. Every time we've sparred, he has thrown just one move and taken me down. I would have thrown dozens at him, all effortlessly blocked or avoided with almost no effort."

"I hear admiration," said Denver.

"Don't you?" asked Melody. "Admire him I mean?"

"He gives me nightmares," said Reg from the back.

"Denver?"

"I admire his control."

"There's more to him than that. We *can* turn him around, but we *all* have to want it."

"Like I said, he gives me the willies," said Reg.

"There's no need. Learn him. Get to know him. I bet if you knew him you'd never feel scared of anything ever again. With someone like him on your side, you wouldn't have to worry about much at all."

"If you wasn't gay, Melody, I'd say you had a crush on him."

"I *can* admire somebody without needing to bring sex into the subject, Reg." She turned to him and smiled.

"Who mentioned *sex*?"

"Right, we're here, the club's around the corner. What's the plan?" asked Denver.

"You two stay here, I'll go in alone." Melody pulled the visor down and began to apply lipstick. She dropped her hair from the elastic tie and let it fall into a cute, bouncy style that rested on her shoulders. She applied a little more makeup to her eyes and cheeks then turned to the two men and said, "How do I look?"

"How did you do that?" asked Reg.

Reg passed Melody an ear-piece from the back, which she fitted before hanging her hair over her ear.

"I'm observing only, remember, but be ready for me."

"Go get em kiddo," said Denver.

She blew them both a kiss, got out of the van and strutted

away, hips swaying from side to side and hair bouncing gently with her stride.

Reg and Denver looked on in disbelief.

The club was laid out well, it was small, so Melody could view most of the seats from the upstairs area, where she feigned being stood up and leaned on the handrail alone, glancing from her watch to the doors. There was a small DJ stand on the far left of the club with a dance floor. A few girls were dancing, but most people were either sat or stood around the high tables.

A long bar ran across the back wall, serviced by five staff. They were all between twenty to thirty years old by the looks of it, and most had some kind of piercing or tattoo proudly on show.

Melody checked the dark areas in the corners of the club, and saw no sign of Harvey; only men in suits with loosened ties and shirts slightly untucked, and women with large handbags. They'd all come straight from work. Drinks were flowing, and the chat was thick. It was a weeknight, so the emphasis was more social than the weekend, which Melody assumed would be busier, more chaotic and with more people dancing.

She casually looked around for Creasey but realised that the woman would be perfectly camouflaged in a place like this, with her expensive skirt suit and heels. Melody considered her own clothes and felt like she stood out like a sore thumb, being in tight black pants and a black t-shirt. She leaned back on the railing and peered down onto the dance floor and seating areas.

Three men in suits stood at a high table talking to one woman in a blouse and skirt. The talk looked serious at first, and Melody focused on trying to read lips and judge the tone of the conversation. The men leaned in to hear the woman talk, then all nodded at once in agreement with what she said.

"Haven't seen you before," a man said, leaning on the rail beside Melody.

She groaned inside.

"Haven't seen you either," Melody replied. She was watching the woman at the table below and carrying out a process of elimination. There were two women who in Melody's opinion could have been Creasey. The woman directly below her with the audience of men, and one that was sat by the bar alone with her back to Melody.

"So, what brings you here? Do you work around here?"

"Yeah, not far," Melody replied without looking up at the man.

"Let me guess," the man stood back and eyed her, "you work in admin, for a local finance company."

"Oh wow, you guessed." Melody hadn't even looked at the man yet, she continued to watch options one and two. Option two by the bar was busy on her phone.

"Okay, let me go deeper, you're not HR, you don't look finance. Are you one of those cute girls that are into IT?"

"No way, how did you do that?" said Melody flatly. She had decided to keep the guy talking to her, it made her look less obvious.

"I wish *our* IT staff looked like you, I'd be reporting problems every day."

"Yeah, I bet you would."

"Are you one of those nerdy girls that watches shows about dragons and likes Lord of the Rings?"

"Oh, I'm a *huge* dragons fan," she replied, "can't get enough of them."

"I bet you watch it in bed on a Saturday morning while you eat breakfast? Let me guess wh-"

"You want to get a drink?" asked Melody.

The man was taken back, "Yeah, sure. I'll get them, what do you want?"

"It's okay, I'll come with you, let's go to the bar and chat."

They made their way down the long curved staircase and walked over to the bar. Melody led to make sure they ended up near option two. She pulled an empty stool out three down from the woman who had long brown hair, loosely curled, and matched the image she'd seen on Sneaky-Peeky. The guy sat next to her.

"What can I get you to drink?" he asked.

"Just a soda water for me."

"Is that *it*? No wine or anything?"

"No, not for me."

"Cheap date," he commented and called one of the bartenders. A girl with piercings in her nose and bottom lip came over. She had a single dreadlock in a bush of thick tangled hair and wore thick black mascara, making it look attractive.

Melody glanced at the options again. Two women had joined option one, and the whole table was laughing and joking. One man had his hand on her hip and was rubbing affectionately. They hadn't just met, they were together. She ruled out option one.

Option two still sat alone, she was messaging somebody on her phone, her eyes barely left the screen. It was only when somebody walked behind her that she pulled the screen to her chest so nobody could see what she was typing. Melody settled on option two but saw no sign of Harvey still.

The drinks came, and the man beside her lifted his beer bottle to cheers Melody. She obliged with a chink of her water bottle.

"I hope you don't mind me saying, but you seem a little distracted."

"Do I?" she said. She was still watching option two.

"Yeah. Shall I just go, leave you to it?"

She turned and looked at him, perhaps for the first time, she couldn't remember. "No, stay, sorry. I thought I saw somebody I knew."

The man seemed eased and leaned his elbow on the bar.

"So, now that I have your attention, can I get your name?"

"Sure, it's Kelly. And yours?"

"Miles."

"Miles? Nice to meet you."

They shook hands and, like most men do when they shake a woman's hand, he gave a limp-wristed version of his usual handshake. Melody didn't expect a bone-crunching elbow jerk, but she liked a little effort put into a greeting.

"So what is it *you* do, Miles?"

"Oh, I'm an underwriter for an insurance firm." He gestured his thumb over his shoulder, which Melody took to indicate he worked in one of the large towers in Canada Square.

"Sounds interesting," she lied.

"It pays the bills," he grinned.

She looked passed Miles as a man joined option two at the bar and pulled up a stool. They shook hands formally; Melody noticed the firm but polite handshake. The man looked European, he wore a dark blue sports jacket with smart jeans and brown shoes. An inch of spotless cuff showed from the sleeve of his immaculate jacket, along with the glimmer of an expensive looking silver watch strap.

The man called the bartender over and ordered two waters, then cast his eye around the club; he settled on Melody's eye and stared. Melody returned the stare with a smile and looked back to Miles. The look fed his ego, and he began to talk seriously with option two.

Melody continued to observe the pair while she made

small talk with Miles. She noticed that during the chat, neither of them smiled. Option two did most of the talking and used her hands to express herself. The man nodded, and his eyebrow raised every now and then. He asked a question, and she replied. He nodded. She sipped her drink. And then the cycle would begin again; question, reply, nod, eyebrow, drink. She was selling.

A group of four people approached the bar, and Melody made a show of moving down to make room for them so they could sit together. She was one seat away from option two.

Miles continued to tell an anecdote about a recent business trip, and Melody slipped the LUCY chip from her pocket and held it between her fingers. Option two's bag was open a fraction, hanging on the back of her stool, and she was distracted typing a message on her phone.

Melody pretended to be listening to Miles and waited for the punchline of his story. She laughed out loud and turned sharply to pick her drink up, purposely knocking it over. The bottle rolled towards option two and the man, and she reached out to stop it. Option two pushed her chair back in time for the bottle to roll off the bar and hit the floor by her feet. Melody slipped the chip into the bag and picked up the bottle. "I'm so sorry, I'm so clumsy. Did I get you wet?"

"No, it's fine," she said dismissively and pulled her chair back to the bar. As Creasey leaned forwards off the stool, Melody caught a glimpse of her phone's screen. The woman straightened up and hit send, then had a curt glance around to see if anybody had seen the message.

Melody turned to Miles, "Okay, I guess that's my cue to leave."

"Already? Okay, well, I don't suppose-"

"Sorry, Miles. You've been fun to talk to, but I have to go."

She began to walk away. He followed.

"Hey, is that *it*? I don't even get your number?"

"Well, how about this? If I come back to this club, and you see me in here again, you buy me another drink. I promise you'll get more than just a number. You win." She gave him her best dirty look. "But, if I don't come back, and you *don't* see me. I win."

"Oh yeah? Tell me more about this prize."

"Well, when you get home tonight, why don't you use your imagination?" She walked off briskly.

As soon as she had left the club she hit the button her earpiece three times, "Reg, you there?"

"Yep, how did it go?"

"I slipped the chip into her bag, but there's no sign of Stone."

"He's still in the car. Hasn't moved a muscle. We did a drive-by, her BMW is parked across the street from where you're walking right now, he must be inside."

Melody glanced around at the empty street. "I'm going to take a quick look."

"Be careful, Melody."

She strode across the street and looked in the back seat and the boot, nobody.

"He's not in there." She carried on walking.

"Oh," said Reg.

"What's up?"

"We'll find out when the time is right. That's what Harvey said."

"His watch."

"That's what he was doing when he opened the car door at the farm," said Reg.

"So where is he now?"

"Harvey or Cartwright?"

"My guess is that they're both back in Loughton," said Denver.

"Pick me up, Creasey has a new client, they're heading to

the farm now, and I think she messaged Cartwright, I want to be there before them."

"Sit tight, we're thirty seconds away," said Denver.

"Another client? It's a bit late for all that, isn't it?" said Reg, "It's one am."

"Yeah, well, if Harvey is on Cartwright's tail, he'll be there too."

TAIL

HARVEY CHOSE OPTION THREE.

He walked to the side of the apartment door, put his finger over the spy hole and raised his hand to push the bell. He heard the jingle of keys close behind the door, and lowered his hand. Men's voices approached from the other side. He looked around and ran the few steps to the cleaning cupboard, stepped inside and pulled the door closed after him, just as the front door opened.

From inside the cupboard, he could see through the crack in the door. Donny and his goon waited for the lift to arrive. He saw Donny's scarred face, it looked worse than he thought it would, and gave Donny an evil look. Once they were inside the elevator and Harvey heard the doors close, he bolted to the fire escape and ran down the stairs.

He ran from the apartment's main entrance before Donny and the big guy had started their cars. By the time Donny and Bruno had pulled out of the car park onto the road, Harvey had turned around and was ready to follow them.

He crept to the end of the road and nosed out. Once they were a safe distance in front, he pulled out behind them.

The Mercedes and Toyota turned into Pudding Lane, so he knew they'd be going to the farm. Harvey drove past the turning and diverted to the spot in the fields he'd found before. He bounced through the terrain with his headlight switched off, feeling the way across the rutted land cautiously. Reaching the copse, he ditched his bike and helmet, then ran across the field in the pitch black. He crawled the last two hundred yards to the spot behind the fence where he'd waited before. He let his breathing settle, but this time he had no intention of sitting and waiting for long.

Donny and the goon's cars were already there. The single door to the barn was open, spilling light onto the small area where the cars were parked. As soon as the goon was out, Harvey would step into action.

Two more cars turned into the long driveway, and Harvey cursed at the lost opportunity. He recognised the BMW as Jamie Creasey but didn't recognise the car behind. It was a Range Rover, and it turned to park next to Jamie. A man stepped out and shut the door.

"A barn? Is this some kind of joke?" he said, as Jamie opened her own car door.

"Not just any barn, Mr Stokes. I can assure you."

"Looks like a barn to me."

Donny had heard the arrival and stepped out of the barn's single door.

"You must be Mr Stokes, welcome." He offered his hand. The man took it and shook it, but kept looking around.

"You're perfectly safe here, Mr Stokes. Nobody knows we're here and there isn't a neighbour for miles," said Creasey.

"Come, meet the girls," said Donny. "You're going to fall in love tonight, Mr Stokes."

"If I wanted to fall in love, I wouldn't be *here*, Mr Cartwright."

"Love is temporary, Mr Stokes," said Donny, smiling as he stepped into the barn.

Harvey watched as the single door was pulled closed behind them. He sat back and waited for the tank moving through the shadows, but couldn't see it anywhere. The team would surely know of the new development, and if they'd been smart and followed Creasey like he'd planned, then they might even call for back up.

Less than an hour later the double doors slid open. A plastic sheet had been laid out on the floor inside, and the digger's diesel engine fired up, coughing black smoke noisily into the air. Harvey watched, waited and planned. Execution was imminent.

Mr Stokes emerged from the single door. He abruptly shook hands with Donny and Creasey and walked to his car.

"Was it what you expected, Mr Stokes?"

"I'm not entirely sure what I expected, Mr Cartwright, but yeah, I can see your little enterprise taking off, given the right exposure to the right people." He began to walk away again. "Of course, you'll need to find somewhere else, this place just won't do."

"Are you suggesting you might know of some potential clients, Mr Stokes?"

"I'm saying you should get in touch when you're not based on a farm. Don't get me wrong, it works, but if you're going to charge seventy-five grand a pop, I imagine people will want to relax with the girls, you know, somewhere stylish, with champagne and more girls serving the drinks. I love the nude thing, by the way, no animosity." He opened the car door. "Anyway, thanks for the evening. Like I said, call me when you're set up properly and we'll see where we can help each other out." He started the engine quickly and pulled away, ignoring the waves from Creasey.

The goon pulled the digger out and turned behind the

building. Harvey waited for Donny and Creasey to disappear. He stepped up with one foot on the fence, and was about to pull himself over when Bruno walked back around the corner into the light.

He was carrying somebody on his massive shoulder. It was Melody. She was limp and hung over his huge body like he was carrying a wet towel from the shower.

"Boss," he called when he stepped into the barn, "we got ourselves a visitor." He dropped Melody onto the plastic sheet and pulled her Sig from his waistband, "She was carrying this."

Donny took the gun from him. "Take a torch, look around."

Creasey joined him, and they both stood over her, "I know *her*, she was stood beside me at the club."

"What club?"

"Marco's, where I'd arranged to meet Mr Stokes."

"Did she come into contact with you?"

"No, wait, yes. She spilt her drink and-"

"Check your bag and pockets."

"What for?"

"For something that isn't supposed to be there."

Their voices were raised, Harvey heard everything from where he sat fifteen metres away.

"Do you think she's police?" asked Creasey.

"I think we got ourselves a new girl," said Donny, smiling. "Strip her and put her in stable six."

The goon walked back into the barn, "No sign of anyone else anywhere, boss."

"Okay, carry on digging the hole, Bruno, get rid of that body."

Bruno was watching Creasey unbutton Melody's shirt.

"Bruno?" said Donny.

"Yes, boss."

Bruno walked back out into the darkness and disappeared behind the building. Harvey now knew that Donny was carrying and watched his every move.

Creasey pulled the chip from her bag, it was the size of a small SIM card.

"Bitch," she muttered.

"I'll take that," said Donny. He threw the chip on the concrete floor and grabbed a hammer from where it hung on the wall with other random tools. He destroyed the chip with three direct hits.

By the time he had vented his anger on the small device, Creasey had stripped Melody to her underwear and was uncoiling the hose from its reel on the wall. As she turned the tap, a stream of cold water spewed from its nozzle. She turned it on Melody who immediately woke and rolled over, holding her head. She covered herself as she stood, but didn't say a word. Donny had her gun raised at her.

"Who are you?" he said.

Melody didn't reply.

"You will tell us," Donny said.

"Maybe she needs a little solitude? That might encourage her to talk."

"Room six is all made up for you." Donny motioned with the gun to the line of doors behind her. "In."

Melody stood resolute. She stared at him. Harvey could see the hatred on her face from where he sat. He felt helpless, without a weapon he stood no chance of helping her against the three of them, all of whom could be carrying.

Melody moved out of sight, and Harvey heard the bang of a door being slammed, then the jingle of keys in a lock.

Donny came back into view and stood beside Creasey in the doorway of the double doors. She turned to him.

"She's not alone. There'll be more, they're onto us," she hissed.

"Calm down, there's-"

"Calm down?" she interrupted. "Don't tell me to calm down, who the hell *is* she? And why does she have a gun?"

"Bruno swept the place. If there were more of them we'd of found them, and no doubt they would have kicked the doors in."

"You're saying she's alone?"

"Maybe, let me think. We can't afford to make any rash decisions. My father used to attack problems with a cool head."

"*You* can think all you like, *I'm* out of here," she said, picking up her bag off the floor, "I won't be back until all this is over."

"*What*?" cried Donny. "You can't *leave* just because of this, you're the one that brought her here, she obviously followed *you*."

"I didn't bring her here, Donny, I brought clients here. Two of them in one night, that's two hundred grand. We should cut our losses and get out while we can. We haven't seen Barney for days, do you think maybe that's why? You think he's been-"

"Jamie, shut up. You're hysterical. Get a grip. No-one will do a thing while we have her, she's our guarantee." Donny smiled cruelly.

"Guarantee, Donny?" she started to raise her voice. "So you're into hostages now are you?"

He walked over to her, they were five metres from where Harvey sat. Donny gritted his teeth while he spoke, "If you leave now, you cowardly bitch, I'll keep every penny. There's four hundred grand in there." He gestured to the kitchen. "If Barney has been caught, he's either dead, or he's not talking, so that's two hundred grand each. You walk, and I'll keep the lot. Your choice." He turned away from her. She stood staring at him.

"I can't do it anymore, Donny." Her voice broke.

"I thought you had more balls than that, Jamie."

Her face was screwed up, not with hate, but with fear. Harvey knew the look. He'd seen it on the faces of his targets, and he'd seen it on Sergio's face before he'd boiled him alive.

"We'll move them tomorrow," he said.

"Where to?"

"I'll find somewhere. We'll torch this place."

"And the cop?"

Donny paused and looked her in the eye. "We'll get rid of her, leave no traces."

Bruno came out from the darkness and went to the stables to get the body.

Donny looked at him and gestured with his thumb as he emerged from the stable carrying the dead girl. "It works, Jamie. You can see for yourself. You heard Stokes, there's potential here. We just need to be more careful."

"I'm *scared*, Donny."

"Of what, Jamie? What is it? Prison? There's no chance of prison. There's two outcomes here, you'll either end up dead or rich. Give me six months."

"Six months? I *can't* take another six months of this, Donny. I'm at breaking point."

"Alright, six months and half of Barney's cut."

"What about Barney?"

"He's out. I just severed the tie."

"What if he grasses?"

"Chances are he's dead already. If he isn't, what's he going to say? He's not likely to just tell the police that he's involved in…" he chose his words carefully, "all this, is he?"

"Six months."

"Six months, or a million each. Whichever comes first."

She nodded faintly in the bright light.

"Go, get some rest. We'll take care of all this." He gestured over his shoulder.

Jamie turned and left. Harvey watched her leave. Bruno was wrapping the girl in thick, blue, plastic sheets. Donny stood looking out into the night as Bruno walked passed him carrying the bundle.

"Good work, Bruno."

"Thanks, boss."

Donny pulled his phone from his pocket, dialled and listened.

"Murray, it's me," he began, "I know what time it is, we have a problem." He listened to the voice, then began in a defensive tone. "*No*, it's not *like* that. No. Just a week, I need to find a new place, it's all on top here, we found some bird creeping around outside with a gun." He lowered his voice to a hiss. "What? You *can't* keep them *here*, we're moving the operations tomorrow. *Jesus*, Michael, have I *ever* let you down? I'm *not* letting you down now, we need to move the girls, I'll have a new address tomorrow, you can deliver them *there*. You're on your way *now*? *Five am*? It's *three* am now, you *can't-*" The man disconnected. "Ah, *Christ*."

Harvey overheard the one-sided conversation but could fill in the blanks. Another batch of girls was two hours away, and Melody was in serious trouble.

Harvey watched as Donny nervously began fingering the scar on his face. He was planning.

If more girls were arriving in two hours' time, the place would be full. Melody would be stuck in there. Donny would need to go and find a new place and leave the farm unprotected. That gave Harvey an opportunity to get Melody out, then he'd wait for Donny to return. But he'd need a weapon.

12

MAN DOWN

HARVEY TAPPED ON THE WINDOW OF THE VW Transporter van and saw Reg nervously jump and turn around. He fumbled for his weapon. Harvey opened the rear door and stepped into the light. The smell of fresh coffee hit Harvey.

"It's me, put it down, Reg."

"Stone," said Reg, he lowered his weapon, "Melody-"

"Yeah, I saw it. I need a weapon."

"A weapon? I'm not sure-"

"We can't give wanted criminals weapons, Harvey," said Denver from the front. He was turned in his seat and faced Harvey. Harvey saw a cool boldness in his eyes.

"You want Melody back?"

"Sure we do."

"Are you two about to go in there and save her?"

"We're not trained for that sort of thing."

"I am, so give me a weapon."

Denver stepped from the van and walked around the back to join Harvey. He held out a hand, Harvey studied him and then shook it.

"You back then?" Denver asked.

"Have you called it in yet?"

"Melody? No, not yet."

"What's your plan?" asked Harvey.

"Whatever it was, rescuing Melody wasn't part of it. We can do this together, Stone."

"Did you hear the phone call?"

"Cartwright's?" said Reg, "Yeah, it's a burner."

"He's the source, the Michael guy. Donny was scared. There's a new batch of girls arriving at five am."

"That gives us a little over one hour," said Reg.

"No, Donny and his goon will need to go and look for new places. They're going to torch this place and move operations."

"Torch it?"

"Fire, Reg," said Harvey, "lots of it."

Reg looked away.

"So, we wait for the delivery," said Denver, "then once Cartwright leaves to find a new place, we go in and get Melody out."

"No," said Harvey, "more detail. The success is in the detail."

Denver and Reg stared at him.

"The girls will arrive in a lorry or truck of some description. The lorry will need to be tracked. Do you have any of those LUCY chips left?"

"Sure," said Reg.

"Okay, your job is to make sure that lorry gets a chip. Once it leaves here, it'll take us right to the source, that'll please Frank."

"Got it," said Reg.

"The girls will be stripped and thrown into the stables with the other girls. The truck will be out of there as fast as possible, they won't hang around. Donny will leave to go see the new place, which he's probably researching right now. Reg, can you tap into the internet in there?"

"It has internet? It's like something from *The Waltons*."

"There's a control room, and cameras in every stable. If you can get the video feed, there's your case right there. That'll also please Frank. Donny will go find the new place, we go in, get all the girls out, I wait inside."

"What?" said Denver.

"I came for Donny. I'm taking him out. He'll come back from the trip, and I'll deal with him. You guys have Jamie on screen still?"

"Yeah, thanks for the clue," said Reg.

"Okay, you keep an eye on her, Denver. She's terrified and won't be back for a while, but if she does come along, you guys take her off the road, put the cuffs on. Frank'll be happy three times in one day. Frank gets Creasey, and the source, Michael, plus the girls live. I get Donny."

"Sounds like a plan," said Denver.

"Plus, Sneaky got the plates of Mr Narakimo, we'll find him, and who's the guy that just left?" said Reg.

"Stokes," replied Harvey. "Two killers, the salesman and the source."

Reg handed Harvey an ear-piece, "Welcome back, Harvey, we missed you," said Reg with a grin.

Harvey fitted the ear-piece. "Reg are you inside that internet yet?"

"Yeah, Donny's looking at nearby commercial rental properties."

"Would the CCTV be on the same network?" asked Harvey.

"If a dumbass installed it, yeah. Why?"

"There's a bunch of screens on the wall in the control room, there's cameras in every stable."

"Okay, well let's see," Reg went into Reg mode and began

to talk to himself as he worked, "cameras are usually UDP based and will require a server or gateway-"

"What's UDP?" asked Denver, regretting the question before he finished asking it.

"That's a good question, Denver. User datagram protocol is a method of transmitting data over the internet that doesn't resend lost packets-"

"Okay, we don't really have time for this, save the IT lesson for when we're back in HQ eh?" said Harvey.

Denver glanced up at Harvey. "You are coming back then?"

"Let's just say my options are open right now," said Harvey.

Denver nodded at him, and they banged fists.

"Okay, if you guys have stopped being so cool, let's do some pinging over ports seventy-five and eighty. Hmm, there's the internet gateway there," he pointed to the screen, "and hello, there's the media server. So, if I browse to the IP address over port eighty, aha." He stopped the muttering. "We have a log in screen, we just need the username and password for the CCTV system. Let's try admin and admin." Reg entered the default credentials, and the screen went blank, then eight small thumbnails appeared with one larger window above showing the Mercedes and Toyota sitting at the front of the barn.

"I'm impressed, Reg, that was under a minute," said Harvey.

"If you teach me how to kill with my bare hands, I'll teach you how-"

"I'm not that impressed, Reg. What's on the cameras?"

"Camera one, front exterior." Reg made a note on his pad.

"Camera two," he clicked the next thumbnail, "an empty room."

"That's stable one, make a note," said Harvey.

"Presumably, this is stable two then," said Reg, making a note.

"Oh dear," he looked up, horrified at the image on the screen. Three girls sat huddled on the single bed, they were naked.

"That's stable three," said Harvey, "stable four will look the same. Melody is in six."

Reg hovered the mouse over the thumbnail for stable six and looked back at Harvey and Denver. They nodded.

Melody was in her underwear, her wrists were bound, and she was working her way around the room looking for weaknesses in the walls.

"Oh, crap," said Reg.

Denver looked away.

"Does she have comms?" asked Harvey.

"Of course, but she went radio silent as soon as she was caught. We don't know if it fell out, or if it was knocked out, or she's just plain too embarrassed to respond."

Harvey and Denver stepped away from the van. They both had a deep respect for Melody, and seeing her in her underwear on a camera somehow felt inappropriate. They stood in the quiet night and looked towards the direction of the farm. It was obscured by the trees that hid the van, but somewhere over there, less than a kilometre away, was their friend, and she was in a world of trouble.

Harvey pushed the button on the ear-piece. "Melody, it's Harvey. Can you hear me?"

They turned to the screen and watched for her reaction. She didn't respond, but stopped feeling the walls and let her head drop between her arms.

"Do you think she heard?" asked Reg.

"Melody?" said Harvey over the comms.

Melody didn't respond.

"Keep your eye on that room, Reg, anybody goes in there

and messes with her, I want to know. We'll put plan B into action."

Harvey reached for Melody's over-sized Peli case and pulled it across the wooden floor. He flicked the two metal catches and opened the lid. Inside was a Diemaco L119A1, along with a laser sight and three loaded magazines. All of the items had the foam insert neatly and precisely cut out around them. The Diemaco was one of Melody's favourite weapons.

"And what exactly is plan B?" asked Denver.

"I kick the door in and tear the place apart." Harvey inserted a magazine and slammed it home, "That will not please Frank," said Harvey.

Harvey was in position behind the fence by the time the lorry turned into the long driveway. It bounced along the potholes, but the driver didn't slow.

It was a four-ton truck with an electric tail lift fitted to the rear and a sliding shutter that rolled up to the lorry's roof. It turned among the cars and reversed up to the double doors of the barn. Clearly, the same driver had delivered the first batch of girls.

Harvey called the plate number over the comms, and Reg ran a search for it.

Sneaky-Peeky sat in the long grass, further back than before as daylight was brightening the gloomy sky. Sneaky gave Reg and Denver a clear view of the front of the barn and was recording; they also had a picture of inside the barn from the cameras.

The driver stepped down from the lorry and banged on the double doors. Harvey placed him in his mid-forties, slightly overweight, but not too much. In his heyday, he would have been a well-built guy. He could probably still handle himself. He had on clean work boots and jeans, with a checkered shirt over a plain white t-shirt. His head was shaved, and a large tattoo reached up from under his collar on the back of his neck; a claw of some kind.

The man's banging was answered by a tired looking Bruno who slid the doors open. The lorry was reversed in halfway by the driver, and the barn's sliding double doors were closed onto the sides of the truck. Harvey presumed this was an attempt to stop any girls from running and to prevent any prying eyes looking in.

He heard the tail lift's motor whine into action, and slowly lower the large metal plate down to the floor. The sound of the shutters being thrown up then started the chorus of whimpering girls.

Another car pulled into the driveway, it was another Mercedes, similar to Donny's but silver.

"Reg you have got eyes on the driveway?" asked Harvey.

"Not yet." Reg hit a button and turned Sneaky's turret. "Unknown, maybe the source? It can't be another client surely."

"Yeah, it's unlikely the main man would travel in a lorry with a load of illegals. Run the plates."

"The lorry is a rental. I could have guessed that, registered in Norfolk."

"The source's Mercedes is registered to a Michael Murray, Ipswich."

"They're bringing them in on the East Coast somehow," said Denver.

"Whoopsie, I just lost the live feed," said Reg.

"They turned the cameras off?" Harvey whispered.

"I can't even hit the router, they turned everything off."

"How about the tank?"

"Sneaky's still running."

Harvey launched himself over the fence and ran to the

side of the building. He took a glance around at the front of the truck that stuck out from the doors and edged closer. He slipped silently to the front of the lorry and fixed the chip's magnetic side to the inside of the wheel arch.

Inside the barn, the shutter was pulled down with a screech, and the tail lifts motor began to whine back into life. Harvey ran for the fence, jumped over it and sank down just as the doors were opened. He peered through the bush. The driver casually climbed in like he had just delivered a bunch of fruit and veg. He started the truck's diesel engine and pulled out of the barn. The driver took even less care as he bounced the truck across the bumpy driveway.

"Reg, you tracking that truck?" he whispered.

"I am, but wait, Melody's moving too with the truck. She's bloody *inside* it."

"What?" asked Harvey. "Repeat."

"Mills is *in* the truck."

Harvey leapt over the fence once more, dropped to the ground and scrambled to the Mercedes. He checked inside to make sure it was clear, then popped the boot lid, climbed in and closed it on top of him.

Reg watched on Sneaky's camera, "Harvey that's not the best idea you've ever had."

"Got another one?"

"Hmmm, no."

"Reg, track that truck, she's going to need you close by in case the truck and car head to different locations."

"You could have just come back here, and we could all drive together?"

"You tracking me?"

"Yeah, your new chip is pulsing on LUCY. It's flashing red, for *crazy fool.*"

"Okay, Denver, I'm going to need you right behind," whispered Harvey.

Harvey heard footsteps approaching the car. He drew his Sig and aimed above him, ready in case the boot was opened. The Diemaco lay by his side, but the barrel was too long to bring up and use inside the tiny boot compartment, plus it would probably deafen him. Harvey heard the driver's door open and felt the suspension take the weight of the man. The heavy door was closed, and the engine purred to life.

Harvey held tight as the large saloon drove slowly along the driveway. He was leaving Donny behind but had little choice. Melody was in serious danger now. At the farm, they always had plan B. In the truck, the scenarios were too numerous to imagine.

Harvey made himself as comfortable as he could and judged his location by the turns of the car. They had turned right out the driveway and had been going straight for some time. When the driver had relaxed into the journey, he turned music on. It was soft, stringed music; something John would have listened to. Harvey didn't know the names of musicians or composers. He didn't have a favourite band. He listened to music when he worked out, and either liked it or he didn't.

The music gave him a chance to contact the boys. He tapped three times on the ear-piece.

"Loud and clear, Harvey." It was Denver. "We are one mile behind you, out of sight, but not out of mind."

"Melody?" he whispered.

"Melody is ahead of you, less than a mile. You're catching her."

"Location?"

"We are on the A12 eastbound heading towards Ipswich."

Harvey didn't reply.

"Harvey, key the mic three times to confirm."

Harvey tapped on the ear-piece three times and settled in for a long ride.

An hour passed slowly.

He felt the car slow but not stop, like it had pulled onto a smaller, slower road.

He tapped three times on the mic.

"You still with us, Harvey?" It was Reg.

His throat was dry and cracked. "Copy," he whispered.

"You want the good news or the bad news?"

Harvey didn't reply.

"Okay, I'll give you the bad news. We're in a place called Mistley, about twenty minutes from Ipswich."

Harvey waited for the good news.

"The good news," Reg continued, "is that the sun is shining, and we're by the seaside. Perhaps we can rescue Melody and then grab an ice cream on the sea-front afterwards?"

"Melody?"

"You're in the lead car, Melody is directly behind you, and we're hanging back one mile."

"You have a plan, Harvey?"

"I always have a plan."

The car stopped, and the driver's door opened. Harvey heard the sound of a gate being opened, then felt the driver return and the car pull inside the gates. The engine was cut. Harvey closed his eyes and tried to picture the scene.

He heard the loud hiss of the truck's air-brakes beside the car, then the muffled voices of the two drivers. He focused. The gates were dragged closed, steel on concrete. The sound of the driver's shoes told him it was a rough concrete floor. There was a faint echo, but also a breeze that blew against the car. He pictured an open-sided warehouse with a large metal roof. Perhaps with a small port-a-cabin for an office or storage. He heard water, softly, and the sound of birds, gulls. Maybe it had been designed to be a place to offload fish.

The whine of the truck's tail lift broke his concentration once more. The screech of the rear shutter bounced around the warehouse. Harvey could place the truck, the water, and the men.

"Get her straight in the boat, Roger," one of the men said, he had a thick country boy accent, "we don't want anybody seeing her. Fuel up, and give me a shout. I'll go get changed, we can do a spot of fishing while we're out there."

"Denver, come back," Harvey whispered.

"Copy, we're outside the gates. You're under a large roof in a compound, I can see the car through the gap in the gates. The truck is next to it, but the shutter's open and we can't see Melody."

"Does this place back onto the water?"

"Yep, I'm looking at satellite imagery," said Reg, "it has a private dock to the rear that leads out to a public beach. One small fishing boat docked."

"Denver, we're going to need to borrow a boat."

"Borrow?" said Reg.

"Melody is being taken out to sea, I think they'll throw her overboard."

"What are you going to do?" asked Denver.

"Adapt my plan," said Harvey. "Let me know when you are floating. Oh, and Denver?"

"Stone?"

"Best make it a fast boat, eh?"

Denver chuckled. "If I'm going to steal a boat, you can bet your ass it's going to be a fast one."

13

DENVER'S DREAM

HARVEY PULLED THE EMERGENCY RELEASE ON THE INSIDE of the Mercedes, and the boot lid raised. He caught it before it had a chance to swing up, rolled out of the car and crouched behind. He reached in and grabbed the Diemaco then lowered the boot lid.

The surroundings weren't far from what he had imagined. He was stood in the centre of a warehouse that was open on two sides. On one end were the gates, which had been locked from the inside. The other end had a small fishing boat rocking gently on the water by the private dock. The concrete floor had channels running front to back every twenty feet, presumably to hose the floor down after it had been filled with fish.

One man emerged from the cabin in the hull of the boat, it was the lorry driver, Roger. He closed the hatch of the cabin and fiddled with something that Harvey presumed was the lock. Harvey ducked low behind the car and watched the man prepare the boat.

"How you getting on, Roger?" a voice called from the far side of the warehouse. "Ready to head off yet?"

"Aye, Mike, that we are," he replied.

Harvey watched the man named Michael walk down from a small wooden hut at the end of the warehouse. He'd changed out of his suit and into yellow waterproof fishing trousers and long rubber boots. He had on a thick woollen jumper. His clean shaved face made him look like he was going to a costume party as a fisherman. His clothes were too clean, and his face too fresh to pull off the seaman look.

Roger, however, did look like a sea-faring man. His red face and thick growth suited the overalls and beanie hat he wore. Plus, he moved around the boat with a casual ease, like he'd been around boats his entire life.

The big diesel engines fired up and idled.

Harvey took aim at the boat. It was within range. The vessel was only thirty feet long. It was white with a central helm under a solid canopy. The cockpit seated two people and the rear of the boat had a bench all the way around it. The door to the cabin in the hull was between the two cabin seats. Fishermen could also walk around on the stern of the boat, where the rail opened up to a small stainless steel platform designed for fishermen to stand on when playing large fish.

Michael untied the bowline knot that secured the craft to the dockside and lifted the fenders up out of the water. Roger expertly turned the vessel in the small space, then surged forwards, maintaining the five miles per hour limit and no wake zone inside the River Stour's narrow estuary.

Harvey didn't have a clear shot, and when the boat powered off, he ran to the water's edge only to see them disappear around a corner.

He glanced up and down the long concrete dock, it had been split into private docks all along, but no other boats were tied up. Further along the dock, in the open stretch of water that led out to the estuary, small boats rocked gently in the calm and protected water. Harvey made his way along the edge of the dock towards the beach.

He jumped down from the concrete harbour onto the stony beach. It was quiet, so he waded out to the first boat he saw with the rifle hidden behind his body as best he could. The cold water bit into his skin like sharp needles. He dropped the weapon over the edge and pulled himself into the boat and lay flat on the floor, then waited a standard minute, soaked and cold.

Harvey forced himself up to his feet and sat in the captain's seat. An ignition switch much like that of a car's was to the right of the helm. No key. Harvey had never stolen a boat before but figured it couldn't be too different to stealing a car.

Harvey searched the boat and found something that would work. An old, heavy fishing gaff with a hollow pole handle similar to a scaffold tube was fixed to the top of the cabin, presumably so the fisherman could reach it from whichever side he was playing fish.

He smashed the fibreglass panel surrounding the ignition with the heavy gaff, then slotted the tube end over the ignition barrel. With a small amount of leverage, Harvey was able to snap the ignition barrel off, which left him with a square hole roughly half an inch wide. A small flathead screwdriver he found on the centre console fit the square hole easily. He turned. The engine tried to turn over but didn't fire into life.

Harvey found the primer, gave it a few pumps and then tried the ignition once more. The heavy engine slowly stuttered, and shuddered into life. Harvey had never driven a boat before so he familiarised himself with the controls. He hit the button on his ear-piece.

"Reg, Denver, copy?"

"Copy, Harvey." Denver's voice was faint and lost in the noise of a loud engine.

"You get yourself a ride?"

"Copy that, Harvey, we are ocean-bound now, and out of the estuary."

Harvey looked out at the estuary but couldn't see them.

"Comms are weak, Harvey-" static rushed across the channel and swallowed Reg's voice, "-away from the van."

Although he missed most of what Reg said, Harvey guessed that the comms relied on the aerial attached to the roof of the van, which was connected to the repeater.

Harvey looked around the cab. Above the captain's seat was a small VHF radio. He switched it on, and it gave several beeps, then the LED screen settled on channel four. He pulled the handheld mic down from its cradle, it hung from a long curled cable like an old telephone handset.

"I'm on channel four," he said over the ear-piece, "do you copy?"

A series of broken signals came back at him loud and sharp in his ear. Then the radio burst into life.

"Broken stone, broken stone, this is Denver's dream, come back."

"Denver's dream, this is broken stone, are you ready to go fishing? Heads up, there may be somebody already in our spot, but I'm sure if we ask nicely they'll move along."

"Broken stone, this is Denver's' dream, we're looking forward to getting our hooks into something big today."

"Not if I hook it first, Denver's dream, out."

Harvey liked Denver, he was switched on. On an unencrypted radio, anybody could be listening; Denver had communicated well.

There were only three controls; two throttles and a wheel, no pedals. Harvey pushed the two throttles forward, and the front of the boat raised up and began to shift forward faster than he had expected. He hung onto the wheel and retained his balance. The boat clumsily turned and leaned over to one side when Harvey turned the wheel too hard to the left and water sprayed out from underneath. The loose items on the boat slid across the deck to one side.

Harvey corrected the move with a turn to the right and, after a few more bumps and splashes, straightened out. He cranked the throttles forward until the engines sounded like they would blow then dropped them down a fraction. Harvey learned to use small corrections of the wheel, and soon he found himself between buoys that led to the centre of the river's estuary, and he sped out to sea.

The choppy open water hit the boat's hull hard. He felt the little boat slam into the water, so he eased down the throttles a little and scanned the horizon for movement. There were plenty of fishing boats and they all looked like the thirty footer Melody was trapped in.

Harvey searched around inside the cabin and found some old binoculars in a plastic case. He killed the boat's engine and stood upon the prow, scanning the boats.

Men were dragging nets, pulling ropes, and casting rods, but none of them wore yellow fishing trousers. He wiped the filthy dirty lenses on his shirt and did another scan of the boats out at sea. One small white boat was moving fast way out beyond the stationary fishing vessels. To the left of it, a fifty-foot cruiser easily cut through the rough, deep water. It was much larger than the fishing boat and held a faster speed.

Harvey was sure it was Denver at the wheel of the cruiser. They were running adjacent to the fishing boat, but not directly in its wake. Harvey stepped down to the helm and slammed the throttles forward. The little engine surged back into life. He pointed the prow at the white fishing boat in the distance and held his course. The hull slammed continuously into the water and shook the entire boat each time.

Tearing between the other fishing boats, Harvey sprayed

surf high into the air above them; he ignored the calls and shouts of angry fisherman. He was locked onto a target.

He left the fishermen far behind; the land became dark, as did the distant strip on the horizon that split the white sky and black ocean. Denver's dream was far out to his left, Harvey guessed it to be a kilometre away. Directly in front of Harvey was the little white fishing boat, maybe two kilometres away. It had stopped and turned side on. Harvey turned right to circle the boat then killed his engines.

The little craft rose and fell with the waves, which made using the binos difficult. Harvey found the boat and focused. Then he looked on with dread. Melody was stood on the side of the deck, her hands were bound. She was dressed in only her underwear and looked absolutely broken. Her posture had lost its usual strong and defiant rigidness; her shoulders hung weak and limp, framed by the frigid sky beyond. The man in yellow rubber trousers had hold of her arm and was shouting at her.

Then he shoved her into the water.

Harvey reached for the Diemaco and took aim. But the ocean swells and the distance made it an impossible shot. He shoved the throttles forwards and aimed at the fishing boat.

He smashed the front glass with the butt of his rifle and turned his head away; fragments of glass bounced off his skin and t-shirt. He took aim through the broken window.

One of the men turned and saw Harvey approaching. He called to his mate, and the little boat immediately took off, leaving Melody in the freezing water, barely able to keep her head above the water.

Harvey took aim, fired, missed, fired again and missed. Too much movement. He closed in and killed the engines, then quickly switched the rifle's selector into burst, and fired off the magazine in groups of three.

The two men remained standing, but black smoke began to pour from one of the engines.

Harvey turned his attention to Melody. He found her, a small dark spot in an already dark ocean. Aiming the boat at her, he slammed the throttles into full once more. As he drew near, she sank lower out of sight. He steered the boat past where she had been moments before, slipped the rifle over his shoulder, and hurled himself into the ocean.

He crashed into the hard water and span beneath the surface, rolling in a world of tiny bubbles. He forced his eyes open and searched around him. Looking down, he saw Melody's bound hands reaching up, sinking further. Harvey turned, kicked and reached, he held his nose and equalised then kicked harder; his lungs screamed. He just needed to inhale, the urge was overwhelming. He told himself one more kick, then another. One final kick and his fingers grazed hers in the darkness. He reached down further and gave every bit of energy his body could muster. His hands found the ties on her wrist; he pulled and straightened up.

Harvey kicked up hard, breathing out the spent air. His legs were burning, his boots and the rifle were heavy, and his clothes dragged in the water, but he kicked harder, faster, urgently, until he finally broke through the surface. Inhaling huge lungfuls of air, he gasped for breath, straining to stay buoyant.

Melody did not gasp for air.

She remained silent with her eyes closed and mouth open, with pale white skin.

Harvey held her head above the water, her skin was ice cold. He waved over to the incoming boat and shouted, "Hurry!"

Melody's hair clung to her face so Harvey brushed it

away. He was fighting to stay afloat, but felt for a pulse, nothing. He felt for her heartbeat, nothing. He breathed into her mouth. The boat was closing in on them. Harvey couldn't perform CPR bobbing up and down in the ocean, it was as much as he could do to keep them both afloat. His breaths into her did little to help, but he wasn't a trained first aider, he was just doing what he could. He pulled her bound hands over his head and lay on his back, kicking towards the boat.

Reg and Denver approached. Reg was stood at the back of the boat on a little platform. Denver killed the engine and expertly coasted to a stop, swinging the rear of the stolen forty-eight-foot game fishing boat towards Harvey.

Harvey held Melody's head above the water, and swam on his back, fighting the current with one arm. He kicked with his heavy boots, but the weight was taking its toll on his legs. Harvey reached for the platform and held fast to one of its handles. He let his aching legs drop into the ocean below and clung to Melody with his free arm. Reg bounded back down to the platform with a blanket he'd found, and helped pull her out. Her skin was shockingly white, and she was cold and weak. Her body had released its energy trying to fight the cold in the back of the lorry, then in the boat, then finally in the water it had given up.

Harvey dragged himself up out of the water onto the platform, slipped the rifle from his shoulder and pulled his wet shirt off. Then knelt beside Melody.

Harvey shouted at Melody, "Come on, Melody, fight." He banged on her chest, tilted her head back and pinched her nose. He gave her one full breath and saw her chest rise as the air filled her lungs.

He moved to her chest and placed the heels of his hands over her heart, interlocked his fingers and straightened his arms. He pumped.

"I heard it's fifteen pumps to one breath," said Reg. He began to pull the blanket over her legs.

"Come on, Melody, help us," Harvey called. He slapped her face, then returned to her mouth and gave one more deep breath.

Reg stood with his mouth open, unable to help, he was mortified. Harvey continued to pump her heart.

"Melody, we need you, you can't leave us now." Harvey pumped. "Twelve, thirteen, Melody hurry up, come on, wake up." Harvey was shouting now. Melody's lips had a tinge of blue around the edges.

Harvey tilted her head back, pinched her nose, and breathed one more full breath into her. Her chest rose and sank as the air escaped, and Harvey returned to pumping her chest, "I can do this all day if I have to Melody, but you are not leaving us now."

A little water spurted from Melody's mouth when Harvey pumped and was immediately followed by retching and coughing. Harvey rolled her onto her side.

"Oh, thank god," said Reg, who knelt opposite Harvey and pulled the blanket over her.

The two men carefully sat her up, then Harvey heaved her up into his arms, stood, and walked her into the cabin, keeping close to her to share his body heat. He laid her down on the long bench that ran along one side of the cabin.

"Denver, do you have visual on them?" asked Harvey as he approached the helm with Melody in his arms.

"They're gone. They headed back to the port."

"We need to get her to a hospital," said Reg.

"I don't need a hospital," interrupted Melody weakly, "I need some damn clothes." She was hugging the blanket around her and breathing hot air down onto her chest. She wiped her eyes and sniffed. Harvey laid her on a bench with a blue, plastic-covered foam cushion.

"Reg, check down below, I'll see what I can find up here. Denver, get us back to shore." Harvey ripped up the other seats and looked inside the storage compartments. He found emergency equipment; flares, first aid and a life raft that looked older than the boat.

Reg stepped up from the cabin below carrying an old sports bag. He bent down next to Melody and spoke softly, "Hey girl, you're in luck. I found a bag of old clothes. It's almost like one of the Kardashians left their overnight bag. Here, look at this, there's a thick woolly sweater, the itching will be a reminder of how fab you look." Melody broke into a smile and an involuntary laugh broke through her tears. "And looky here, these are simply stunning darling, the latest line of knock-off Nike tracksuit bottoms. And last but not least, thick, woolly socks. Boy, does this guy like his wool, and look at the size of them," he held the sock up, "Melody, you could literally curl up inside that." She laughed again and he handed her the bag.

"Can you help me?" She wrapped the blanket tight around her and lifted her arms. Reg fed the thick sweater over her and pulled her arms through so she could pull the top down. Melody pulled the blanket away from underneath. Reg opened up the tracksuit pants and helped her feed her feet into the holes then helped her with the socks, which were far too big and slippery on the deck, but she needed the warmth, so kept them on. She pulled the blanket back around her and dried her hair with it, then pulled her knees under her chin on the bench seat, and closed her eyes.

"Should she be sleeping?" asked Denver, "Isn't it dangerous or something?"

"Leave her be," said Harvey, "we need to find her a hot shower-"

"And some decent clothes," Melody added from under the blanket. "I look like a Russian hobo."

The three men all smiled, Melody would be okay.

"We can't go back to the same port in a stolen boat," said Denver.

"Yeah, I made a few locals mad," said Harvey. "Probably not a good idea. What *happened* to my boat?" he looked around the horizon, there was no sign of it.

Denver was looking out to sea. "You leave the throttles open?"

"Yeah, wasn't time to park it." Harvey smiled. He looked down at the ignition by the wheel, expecting to see similar damage to what he had done to his stolen boat, but there was no damage. "How did you do that?" he asked Denver casually.

"Do what?"

"Start the engines without damaging the ignition."

"I'll teach you someday," said Denver. He turned the wheel, and gently slid the throttles forward. The boat responded, and soon the rhythmic lull of the hull cutting through the ocean swells sent Melody off into a deep sleep.

Harvey stripped the Diemaco and the Sig and cleaned them as best he could with whatever rags and tools he could find. Reg was lost without his tech, but sat by Melody and held her steady in case she was thrown from her seat on the rough seas.

When Harvey was done, he stood next to Denver who was navigating a different river estuary looking for a safe place to ditch the boat. Many of the smaller docks had security that would question why three men and a girl might arrive at a dock with no identification in an ensemble of clothes and an automatic weapon.

He found a marina that looked nearly empty of life and pulled the throttles back to neutral, letting momentum carry the boat forward. He gave a slight tickle of one engine to push the boat into the dockside. Harvey had kicked the fenders out and was ready with the rope when the boat gently nudged the concrete. Harvey tied a neat bowline and reached down to help Melody out.

The rifle was wrapped in the blanket, much to Melody's annoyance, and they walked up the path towards the main road where a security guard came from out of nowhere and stood before them. "Good morning, can I see your paperwork please?"

"Paperwork?"

"Paperwork. Boat registration-" He hadn't even finished his sentence when Harvey's arm came thrusting out from under the blanket, hard and fast. The man's legs turned to jelly, and he crumpled to a heap on the ground.

"Let's move, now."

The four moved fast towards the road. It was quiet, so they walked away from the little port, heading north.

"How did you do that?" asked Denver.

"Do what?"

"He's unconscious. How you do that so quick?"

"I'll teach you one day." Harvey grinned at him.

14

TRAFFIC

THE TEAM WALKED SIDE BY SIDE INTO THE SMALL TOWN OF Brightlingsea. It was the first time they'd been together and on the same team for what was essentially only a few days, but it felt like weeks.

They flagged the first cab they saw and rode in near silence northbound back to Mistley; it was a twenty-five-minute journey made longer by the early morning traffic and the cab driver's reluctance to use first or third gears. Denver struggled to contain his frustration at the man.

The Diemaco lay across melody's knees wrapped in the blanket. Harvey sat in the front. They drove past the VW Transporter and asked the driver to stop five hundred yards further along the road. The gates of the warehouse looked closed and locked, but they wanted to be sure. Denver walked back on foot and drove the van to pick them up while Reg, Melody and Harvey stood off the main street.

"How does it look?" asked Harvey. "Any sign of life?"

"Heard some banging, but couldn't see anything. The Mercedes was gone. I could see it through the gap in the gates earlier, but not anymore, just the truck."

Reg opened the rear door and began to climb inside, he was already firing up the computers.

"Hey wait," began Melody, she looked at all three of the men in turn, "I just wanted to thank you all. For what you did." She looked humbled but grateful. "You all saved my life back there, each of you, and I can't put in words-"

"We only did what you would have done for us, Melody," said Harvey.

"That may be so, but hey, I have to tell you how I feel. It's the way I was raised." She hugged Harvey, turned to Reg, smiled and put her arms around him, then gave Denver a hug. "I'm just glad we're back as a team now. We missed you, Harvey."

Harvey looked directly at her but said nothing.

"We done with all the loving?" asked Denver. "We've still got two men to find."

"Donny and Bruno?" asked Harvey.

"No, Michael and his friend, Roger, first. Donny comes after," said Melody. "They can't be too far away."

"The longer we take looking for them, the further away Donny gets," said Harvey.

"But we're right here, Harvey."

"Yeah and they're right there," said Harvey pointing back inland, "but for how long?" He stepped back from the van.

"You're *going* again?" said Melody, almost hurt. "We only just got you back."

Harvey didn't reply.

"You can't *keep* quitting on us," she raised her voice at him.

"I have to do this, Melody," replied Harvey flatly.

"Harvey, come on, man," pleaded Denver, "help us take these two clowns down, and we'll *all* go and get Cartwright with you. Surely we're stronger as a unit?"

"Where are they now?"

"Who?"

"The country bumpkins."

"I don't have any information other than the chip on the lorry, and that's in the compound five hundred yards away."

"You don't have their phones' GPS?"

"We don't have their names or numbers yet," said Reg flatly. "I can get them in a few minutes, from Cartwright's phone."

"I can take Donny down and be back here in a day, it'll take you that long to find your two guys."

"Yeah, with collateral damage," said Melody. "If you leave now Harvey that's it. I don't understand *why* you'd throw all this away, look at us, we're a great team."

"I'm not asking you to *understand*. I'm telling you I'll be away for one day."

"What do we tell Frank? I have to check in soon," she lied.

"I don't care what you tell Frank."

Melody climbed into the passenger side and pulled the door closed. Reg sat down in his seat, and Denver walked to the driver's door shaking his head.

Harvey watched the van start and pull away from the curb. It disappeared around the corner, and Harvey was left alone holding the Diemaco bundled inside the blanket, with a wet shirt and boots.

He carried the bundle in the crook of his arms and walked in the opposite direction until he found a bench to sit on. He needed a plan. Sitting on a main road in a wet t-shirt with a military grade weapon wrapped in a soggy blanket wasn't a good place to start.

He needed to find a car, preferably something old, but fast.

Denver stopped the VW outside a small house with a bed and breakfast sign outside. Melody hopped out with her pack and walked casually to the door. She was greeted by a middle-aged lady who looked her up and down with compassion.

"I'm so sorry to bother you, but my friends and I were just in our boat, and I fell overboard. We have a long drive back to London, and I was hoping to have a shower and change my clothes." She held the bag up and gave her best feminine smile.

"Oh you poor thing, come on in here." She ushered Melody into the house, who looked back and winked at the two men in the van. "Are those your friends?" the lady asked.

"Yes, *they* didn't get wet, they're okay. I'll pay full price, I don't mind, I-"

"I wouldn't dream of it, get yourself up to room three, first floor. There's towels on the bed." The lady had a mother's kind but instructive tone. Melody turned back to Denver and Reg and gave a thumbs up. "Do your friends want to have some coffee? It's quiet this time of year, and I have a full pot."

Melody signed the international hand sign for a drink and pointed in the house with her thumb. The van doors were open and closed before she'd turned back around. She headed up the stairs and heard Reg and Denver's voices greeting the old lady as she closed the door to room three.

The bedroom was small but cosy, the type of place her nan might have liked to stay on holiday. The bathroom was clearly a refurb, with exposed plumbing and a small shower stall, toilet and washbasin laid out in an efficient use of space. It was everything somebody would need for a short stay on the coast.

The water was hot, it was everything melody needed right then. Her fingers came back to life as the blood began to flow freely and her skin revelled in the steam.

She dressed in the clothes she carried in her pack.

Overnighters were frequent for the team, so the spare clothes stayed in the van. Reg and Denver also both had packs in the back but chose not to change.

Melody pulled on socks, cargo pants and a clean, tight t-shirt, then pulled her Norwegian sweater over the top, and finished with her pumps. She didn't have spare boots, but they were better than the hideous over-sized socks Reg had found on the boat.

By the time she walked down the stairs, she felt brand new and found the kitchen where they all sat. Reg was in the middle of an anecdote about a childhood seaside visit. Melody hoped it wasn't the one where he had rigged the slot machine to empty its quarry and been escorted back to his parents by the local police.

"You think it's time to head off?" she asked the two men.

"Oh dear, that's better, look at you *now*, such a pretty girl," the old lady began. "Here, I've made you some toast-"

"Oh, I-"

"Come on, I won't hear another thing said about it, sit down. Do you drink tea or coffee? I always find tea makes me wee a lot."

Reg sat with his back to the lady and smirked.

"Coffee please, that'll be lovely. What do we call you ma'am?"

"Sorry, dear?"

"What do we call you? What's your name?"

"Oh, you can call me Dot, Dot Glass."

"Is there a Mr Glass?" asked Denver, being polite.

"No, he buggered off *years* ago, about the time I had the change, you know?" She looked at Melody with raised eyebrows. "Couldn't take the heat."

Reg had his lowered his head and was visibly shaking trying to control his laughter.

They eventually left the house with full stomachs and

Melody was warmed through. They climbed into the van and Reg fired up LUCY. "Right now I don't know if we're catching evil villains or if we're off to bingo," he said.

"Catching evil villains, Reg. Can you get the boatyard on satellite?" replied Melody. "Let's get back into this." She turned in her seat as Reg zoomed in on the warehouse. "Is this live?"

"No, there's around ten to twenty seconds delay depending on the location of the satellite," said Reg.

The little boat was sat at the dock once more. But there was no sign of life. Any activity would be under the huge metal canopy.

"I need to get inside," said Melody.

"Melody you've been dead *once* today already, can't you just relax," said Reg. As he said it, a silver Mercedes nosed out of the side street in front of them. It pulled off and headed away from the dockside.

"Did you guys see that?" said Denver, he was already starting the van.

"Reg, do you have anything on that Mercedes?"

"Only that it belongs to Michael Murray. I have no phone, nothing yet, tried to get it earlier, but couldn't get onto Cartwright's phone."

"The new Mercedes pretty much all have inbuilt GPS," said Denver. "Can't we somehow find the-"

"Serial number of the radio unit using the vehicle's plate number to find the chassis number," Reg cut in, "to find the model of radio, and then find the satellite identifier via the dealer's database? Yeah, we could do that, but I'll need to tap into my control centre back at HQ."

"You can do all that?" asked Melody.

"Already on it. All electronic devices with any form of network connectivity essentially use the same technology, and most of them come from the same few factories in Asia. The chassis number will be linked to the other electronics in the vehicle, probably in some kind of database in the dealership. So I if can tap into that database, I'll find the chassis number and linked devices."

"You ever done that before?" asked Denver.

"No, but it's much the same as any other database. Okay, here we go. I have the device's GPS identifier, I'm just initialising a remote session into HQ to find the right satellite. The scanner on the van doesn't have the range or the power."

Melody turned in her seat to watch him dart around the screens, "You seriously taught yourself how to to do all this?" she asked him.

"Well, yes and no really," he said without stopping or looking up, "I taught myself how to do it all, but the Ministry of Defense kept catching me. I had to find new ways to achieve the same results, so essentially they taught me how not to do it."

He looked up at her and smiled his best childish grin.

"Right, okay, I'm in-"

"You found the serial number already?" asked Melody, shocked at the speed at which he worked.

"Not only have I found the serial number of the stereo, Melody, my friend, but I have targeted the stereo via the inbuilt GPS and found the Bluetooth identifier that is currently connected. I searched the devices with that range of identifiers, each manufacturer of Bluetooth devices would have a range of serials allocated to them for a batch of devices," he explained, "then I found the phone's UID, and its own GPS signal and I am now looking at...." He turned the screen to Melody. "Mr Murray's mobile telephone." He sat back and put the keyboard on the bench and smiled. The screen showed a live view of the iPhone. The other screen showed LUCY's satellite image of both the car's and the phone's GPS.

"We're joining the A12. If you have eyes in the sky, Reg, I'll hang back. Don't want to scare him off."

"Good call, Denver," agreed Melody.

"He's picking up speed anyway, we can't tail him without drawing attention to ourselves."

"You think he's going back to the farm?" said Reg.

"Well, he just got shot at by a nutter on a boat, and his own boat's out of action. If you just delivered a lorry load of illegally imported girls to an underground prostitution ring, and then got your boat shot at, what would you do?" said Melody.

"I can honestly say I've never considered it, Melody," said Reg.

"He's going to be questioning the security of his phone. So he probably won't make a call that will incriminate him," said Denver.

"Right," agreed Melody. "But he's mad as hell because-"

"The girl Cartwright asked him to dump in the ocean-" said Denver.

"Was just rescued by the men in boats that shot at him," said Reg.

"*And* put his boat out of action, right?" finished Melody. The team all came to the same conclusion. "Murray is heading to the farm for sure, he knows we're onto them all, and wants his cash so he can run."

"Sever the ties," said Reg. "Except, we've got the footage of him at the farm from Sneaky."

"We have footage of him getting out of the truck and walking into the barn, we don't have anything that will put him away," said Melody, "Prosecution wouldn't stand up."

"What do we have?" asked Denver.

"We have Cartwright, Brayethwait, Creasey and Bruno Mason. Bang to rights," said Reg from the back.

"Yeah but Harvey isn't going to leave us much of Cartwright, if anything," said Melody.

"And he'll probably need to take Mason down too, to get at Cartwright," said Denver.

"So we have Brayethwait and Creasey," said Melody.

"We also have Mr Narakimo," began Reg "in the same video as the Bruno guy wrapping the dead girl in the plastic sheet. Same for Stokes."

"They'll get murder for sure, the bodies will be exhumed, and they'll find DNA."

"It's not enough," said Melody. "We've been gone more than two days, I'll need to call Frank today, and he'll want more than just two customers, plus Brayethwait and Creasey."

"He's going to need the source, the board won't be happy otherwise."

"Exactly," said Melody. "Let's also offer him a dozen girls' lives."

She dialled Frank's number and straightened in her seat. Her eyes were fixed on the silver Mercedes a thousand yards in front of them.

"No answer, he always picks up," she said to herself and the team.

"It's eleven am. He'll be at HQ for sure. He's going to want a game plan, so how about this, we wait for Murray to get into the barn and incriminate himself, taking the money should do it. Reg can you get eyes inside the barn?"

"If they turned the internet back on, yes, but Cartwright's moving the operations right?"

There's no way anyone can make a deal on a commercial unit, sign the paperwork, hire a lorry, and move the girls to a new place in-" she checked her watch, "eight hours."

"What would you do?" asked Denver.

"Find somewhere close? Maybe he knows someone, he's from the area," said Melody. "How about you?"

"Well, personally, I'd rent a truck, keep the girls in the back until I found somewhere more permanent," he said, "park it up some place nobody goes." Denver shrugged his shoulders, "He knows someone's on to him, and he's a fool if he thinks that killing you is going to stop whoever we are."

"Of course," said Melody, "that's why I was driven all the way out to the sticks, they knew you'd follow, and he'd have time to get the lorry and move the girls. *Damn*." She slammed the dashboard. "Stupid. Why didn't we question *why* I was being moved?"

"We were worried about *you*, weren't until we saw you being put on the boat that we had *any* idea of what they were going doing to do to you."

"Okay we need a new plan," said Melody. "Even if Murray meets Cartwright at the barn or wherever, and takes cash off him, it won't stand up. It's just cash, right? There's no context."

Just then, Denver swerved into the outside lane, and the sound of a roaring engine filled the space inside the van.

"What the-" cried Reg, barely managing to hold onto his bench.

"It's the truck," called Denver, who then dropped a gear and pushed ahead. The truck swerved into the back off the van and caught the bumper, which was pulled off and crumpled under the truck's wheels. Denver fought to keep straight and had to ease off the throttle to stop the tail end bouncing around. The truck slammed hard into the rear of the van. Reg flew off his chair, and the back window shattered glass over him; he curled into a ball and protected his face.

Melody snatched her seat belt off, turned and pulled her weapon. "Stay down, Tenant," she shouted over the racket of the road, engines and screeching tires. Denver was swerving all over the road to try and force the truck driver to make a mistake. Melody aimed over the back of the seat and fired three rounds. The first hit the windscreen and the last two found the truck's radiator. Steam billowed out, but the driver gave one last attempt before the engine blew, he slammed the heavy truck once more into the smaller van.

They felt the van tilt onto two wheels, Denver felt the weight shift on the steering wheel and accounted for it with a sharp, jerky steer. The van came crashing back down on four wheels. Once more Denver fought to keep control but saw traffic stopped dead ahead. He slammed on the brakes and pulled the van off the road, narrowly missing a tanker lorry stopped dead in the slow lane.

They was a huge crash of twisted metal and broken glass as the truck behind them slammed into the back of the lorry. The truck stopped dead, the driver smashed his face on the steering wheel, and the fibreglass sides of the truck's cargo space tore open with inertia, crashing down around the tanker.

Denver took the van down the steep embankment. The vehicle bounced on the rough ground, and the long grass scoured the underside. The van broke through a wooden fence that lined farmers' fields and came to a stop in the dirt.

Melody was out of the van immediately. She tore up the embankment and along the shoulder past people who had climbed out their cars to see the commotion behind.

The passenger side of the truck was embedded in the rear end of the tanker. The driver was slumped over the wheel. Melody had her Sig aimed at the man and walked cautiously around to the driver's side. Cars were stopped in the traffic beside her, they'd been lucky not to have been hit by the wrecked truck. A man in a suit was climbing out his car and froze when he saw Melody's gun. A family in a saloon behind him sat perfectly still, just their heads and eyes followed her.

She approached the man slowly, then sniffed the putrid air. She saw the steady dripping of whatever fuel was in the tanker pooling on the tarmac. The tanker's driver was stepping down rubbing his neck. Denver emerged on the other side of the tanker, Melody saw him through a small gap between the vehicles. "Denver, clear the area, fuel."

Denver looked at the puddle of fuel on the floor, it was trickling backwards and had formed a stream underneath the truck.

Denver heard Melody yelling at the family to get out of the car, he ran forwards banging on car windows. "Get out of your car, sir." He had his weapon drawn and had pulled his vest over his t-shirt when he left the van. "Come on, everyone out, out of your cars."

People were reluctant at first, but when the first few men and women began to emerge from their cars and huddle together on the side of the road, a few more followed like sheep. "Not *there*, away from the tanker, get away from the tanker into the fields." The crowd of people began to move quickly down the embankment and through the broken fence. A young girl was crying and stood alone next to her family's car with her thumb in her mouth.

Denver rushed to her, scooped her up and bolted down the embankment. A worried mother held her arms open to take the girl off him, the husband stood beside her holding a baby. Neither said thanks to Denver, but he knew that under pressure, most humans went into self-preservation mode before group preservation mode. The girl was mad at them for leaving her but hugged the woman who was stifling her tears.

There were close to one hundred people stood along the foot of the embankment looking up at the carnage. Denver ran up to the road and waved his hands, indicating that everyone should go back further. The crowd paid attention and slowly walked back into the field.

Melody had cleared the cars from the fast lane and edged back towards the ruined truck. The driver was groggily lifting his head, he was dazed and looked around him. He rubbed his face and winced when he found glass in his forehead.

"Get down from the truck, Roger."

"Who the hell are you?" he asked, his voice was weak and tired.

"Get down from the truck, and I'll explain, but right now you're sitting on a time bomb, the tanker could go any minute."

He looked down at Melody's gun, at the tanker then at where he was.

"My legs," he began, "they're stuck. Crushed."

"You need help?"

He was fighting the pain, Melody could see it on his face.

"So you can arrest me and jail my crippled ass?"

"Let me help you down, we can-"

"No, shut up," he spat, "it's over."

"What are saying, Roger?" said Melody. "Nothing's over yet."

He reached into the inside pocket of his jacket with his right hand, his left hand hung uselessly by his side. He took a cigarette and placed it between his dry and cracked lips.

"It's over for me." He lit the cigarette. Melody began to move away from the fuel at the sight of the flame.

He took a drag on the cigarette, inhaled deeply then slowly exhaled through his nose.

Then he looked down at Melody, blinked once, and flicked the cigarette through the open windscreen.

15

INSIDE MAN

HARVEY CAME TO THE TOP OF PUDDING LANE IN THE stolen BMW. It was an old model without an immobiliser, from the days when stealing a car was easier than finding somebody's address. These days, cars were harder to steal but finding someone was simple with the internet. Finding people was one of Harvey's specialities. Stealing cars wasn't.

It was early afternoon when he turned into the lane which was typically empty. He approached the driveway of the farm, dropped into second gear, turned and lifted the clutch. As he tapped the gas, the rear end slid out taking him neatly into the driveway sideways but at speed. He skidded to halt and dipped the clutch when he saw the silver Mercedes parked at an angle beside the barn.

The BMW's exhaust grumbled as the engine idled. Harvey planned.

He slipped the gearstick into first and popped the clutch with a healthy amount of throttle. The rear wheels span in the dirt, and Harvey fought to keep the car straight as it bounced across the bumpy track.

He was halfway up the driveway when he saw the first

sign of smoke coming from the barn. Then he saw a figure dart from the barn to the Mercedes. Harvey stopped the BMW four hundred yards from the Mercedes. The two German cars sat facing each other across the desolate stony soil.

Smoke began to billow out from one side of the barn, thick and black, as the blaze took hold of the old wood.

Harvey let Murray make his move first. He was patient, he planned and when Murray put his foot down, Harvey executed.

The large Mercedes fishtailed onto the driveway spraying up dirt and stones across the front of the barn.

Harvey lifted the clutch and span his rear wheels.

Murray steered the Mercedes onto the rough track heading directly at Harvey.

The torque of Harvey's BMW and the power from the rear wheels on the loose surface sent the car crabbing along the drive, its tyres fighting for purchase. Harvey slammed the gearstick into second, and floored the throttle again.

Murray held fast, the gap was closing.

Harvey hit third gear and pulled his Sig.

Murray's view ahead was obscured by dust brought up from Harvey's wheels. He could see the front of the BMW as it approached.

For a split fraction of a second, he saw Harvey's face. Then he saw the gun hanging from the driver's window.

Harvey fired.

Murray snatched the wheel right, and the front of the car left the track. The nose of the BMW slammed into the rear quarter of the Mercedes, tearing off the bumper and shunting the rear wheel into the chassis, crippling the car.

The Mercedes span once before the front right wheel dug into a pothole and lifted the left side of the vehicle into the air. The Mercedes slammed down on its roof and rolled twice before coming to rest in a hiss of steam and smoke in the long grass beside the perimeter fence.

The front left corner of Harvey's much older and stolen BMW tore clean off on impact with the larger, newer and better-built Mercedes. The car span immediately, slamming Harvey's head hard against the door frame, the force of the spin pulled Harvey left then right again until he slammed once more into the door.

The spin stopped when both the front and rear right-hand wheels dug into the soft earth, and the car flipped over. It rolled once, twice, then after the third roll, it landed with a hard crash on its roof. The wheels turned uselessly in the air.

There was a silence in the driveway. Just smoke and steam rolled across the barren wasteland.

Harvey hung upside down and dazed in his seat belt. Blood dripped from a long wound across his forehead.

The creaking of another car door nearby brought Harvey's focus back from the spinning and rolling and crashing. He reached for his knife, which was permanently in the case fixed to his belt, and cut the fabric of the seat belt. He crashed down onto the inside of the car's roof.

Feet were approaching, upside down, they staggered through the long grass towards him.

A gunshot rang out, then another. It was loud in the silence.

More shots, louder, closer.

Harvey pulled his legs back and kicked out hard at the passenger window. It took two kicks to shatter the glass into tiny fragments that fell around his legs. He shuffled awkwardly towards the window legs first until they found ground. More gunshots nearby. One shot hit the dashboard and ricocheted through the windscreen, shattering more glass onto him. He scrambled faster and rolled free of the car into the long grass. There was a figure on the driveway to his left two hundred yards away. The upturned BMW stood between Harvey and Murray, who was now returning fire at the other person.

Harvey checked around, one end of the barn was fully ablaze, the furthest end. Harvey staggered towards it, the girls would perish in the smoke before the fire reached them. Sirens sounded far off in the distance. Black smoke belched across the land obscuring Harvey's view of Murray and the other figure. Harvey turned and ran as best he could towards the barn.

He broke the single door in with the heel of his foot; it swung back and crashed into the wall behind. He aimed his Sig and stepped inside. Smoke stung his eyes and tore at his throat, he lifted his shirt up to cover his face. He needed to act fast. He kicked the door to stable six in and swept the room with his weapon. It was empty. In the main room of the barn, the far wall began to crumble, as its old dry timber was eaten by hungry flames.

He kicked in the door to stable five, it was empty, then continued along, kick, sweep, check, move along. Stables three and four had a single bed in the centre of each room and a rancid bucket that had been used for a toilet. Stable two had nothing, he approached stable one knowing it would be empty. The heat from the burning wall next to stable one was excruciatingly hot. He held his arm up to protect his face, and kicked the door in, nothing.

The kitchen and control room was at the far end of the barn beside stable six, he ran to the door and slipped inside. Everything was gone, the screens, the computers, everything had been removed. He turned to walk out, but as he spun around, a burning wooden beam that had run the length of the barn up in the eaves came crashing down and smashed into the partition wall of the kitchen, blocking his exit. He tried to pull debris from the wall out of the way to escape, but the beam had trapped the gypsum boards beneath its immense weight. Smoke began to fill the tiny space inside the ruined kitchen.

Harvey moved back and looked around him. The kitchen was against the rear of the barn where there were no windows. The exterior wall was far too thick to smash through. He coughed with the smoke, but tore the cupboards from the wall and revealed the gypsum partitioning, then began to kick his way through. He found a gap between the wooden studding that formed the frame of the partition and smashed through it urgently.

He'd managed to break through one side when more of the burning wood fell into the barn outside the kitchen. Harvey felt the heat suddenly increase, the fire was even closer now, he had only a few minutes before the ceiling gave way.

The smoke had also increased. He fell to his knees and sought the layer of cool, clean air on the cold concrete, but there was none. He rolled and sat on the dirty floor, blood from his head wound ran into his eye, and he wiped it with his arm, leaving a red streak across his face.

In front of him, he'd broken through one side of the thick partition wall. He weakly raised his leg and began to kick, but he hadn't the strength. The urge to roll onto his side, curl up and close his eyes was overwhelming.

More timbers crashed onto the floor outside, and a huge dust cloud joined the smoke inside the small space. The ceiling began to buckle with the heat.

Harvey gritted his teeth and searched deep inside himself. One kick at a time, he brought his leg back, growled with fear, fury, anything he could, and smashed his heel into the gypsum in front of him. Again and again. On his fifth kick, he felt the gypsum give way, then his sixth broke through.

The heat from the smashed kitchen doorway was intense.

His eyes stung from the smoke and blood.

He'd made a hole as large as his foot, but moved his face to it and breathed, it was still smoky but felt cooler. He pulled his arm back and punched in the plaster around the hole, working his way around, making the hole larger with each punch.

Then he plunged his head and body through the hole and dragged his legs through just as the ceiling came down inside the kitchen. He lay on the floor, but he wasn't clear of danger. Devastation was happening all around him, and the smoke was growing thicker.

He looked up from the floor, he was in stable six. He'd closed the door behind him when he'd kicked it in earlier, and was now trapped in a larger room with high walls and no ceiling. The exposed roof trusses above were obscured by thick black smoke and the shimmer of the heat. Flames licked out at the fresh wood above him from inside the main barn.

Harvey touched the door handle tentatively, it was red hot. There was no way he was getting through the door. As he turned to find more options, the barn's burning wall fell to the ground with an almighty crash, followed by a searing roar of flames that licked at every empty space in the barn. Harvey heard the suck of air into the fire's lungs, and the heat intensified even more.

The blood continued to run across his brow, he wiped it across his forehead; it seemed to be getting worse. He heard the crack of timber as the weight of the fallen side wall began to pull on the three remaining walls. A small crack appeared between the timbers behind him. The exterior wall was opening. If it came down in the room, it would crush him and destroy the partition that separated him from the fire. His eyes were watered by smoke and blood from his head wound. He kicked at the timbers around the crack until the small break became big enough for his arm.

It felt cool outside, and he lingered there. He searched around one more and pulled a large, six by four timber through the hole from the kitchen. He smashed the end of it into the crack, which widened it a little but not enough. So he jammed the timber in at an angle and heaved on it levering the crack. It was working, but it would surely bring the wall down. He had to carry on, the timing would need to be perfect.

Harvey readjusted the lever and pulled back on the timber, when the wall finally caved in, the rest of the roof would drop, and he'd have moments to escape before being crushed and burned alive.

The crack was widening. Harvey studied it. He looked at the ceiling hanging lower as he levered its supporting wall away. The partition wall behind him was bulging with heat and browning with the fierce fire it was holding back.

He heaved, just once more; it was final. He heard a loud splinter and fell forwards with the timber, throwing himself into the crack. It was wide enough for his torso, but he couldn't pull the rest of his body through. If the wall fell now, he'd be cut in half. He forced himself back inside and tried another angle, and was stuck fast. The timbers cut into his leg, and splintered shards of hundred-year-old oak jabbed into his thigh. Harvey reached down to the ground outside and grabbed hold of whatever he could. Thick bunches of long grass came out the ground in his hands, he scooped bigger bunches of grass, then pulled. The skin on his thigh split, the wooden shard connected with bone. Harvey growled and pulled, harder than before, harder than he knew he could. The shard snapped off its timber inside his leg and fell to the ground.

Harvey rolled away, sucking the cool air into his lungs and heard the sound of twenty tons of aged oak crash into the fire below. There was a whoosh of energy as the fire raised higher in a display of power.

He crawled across the ground, across the soft patch of fresh earth where who knows how many bodies had been hidden, to the fence that ran along the rear of the property. Harvey slipped between the horizontal bars to the relative safety of the field. Cool air licked his scorched skin like a puppy licks its owner.

The sound of sirens outside came loud and true over the roar of the blaze, but the thick smoke from the destroyed barn blocked any visibility.

His leg throbbed and his head pounded from the crash and the smoke.

He gripped the long shard of old oak that stuck from his leg like a mummified compound fracture and felt the searing stab of nerve endings screaming through his limbs. Without releasing his hold, he growled, gritted his teeth and pulled on the shard. With each inch of wood that came out, the pain subdued, until finally, he was able to drop the huge splinter onto the ground and lay back, panting with exhaustion.

Another wipe of blood from his eye brought firefighters into his vision. Hoses and fire trucks had surrounded the blaze. Blood ran from his leg in pulses with his heart; his entire right leg was soaked with sticky red blood.

Harvey grit his teeth once more, and tried to stand. Keeping his right leg straight, he managed to get himself upright and winced as he began to limp through the field. Anxious not to be seen by the firefighters, he tried to hurry. But pain and fatigue overcame the desire to remain unseen, and he strode as best he could through the dry mud.

Eventually, he fell through the trees and clung to his bike. He was able to perch on the seat and look at his leg.

His t-shirt sleeve was ripped, so he pulled the tear and wrapped the fabric loosely around his leg. Then, with his knife, he made a small cut in the inside of his jacket, which still hung on the bike handlebars where he'd left it, and tore out some of the cotton wadding that lined the pockets. He placed that between the material and his leg and tied the homemade field dressing tight.

Harvey pulled on his helmet carefully, avoiding the sliced skin across his forehead, then faced the challenge of getting onto the bike. His leg was too painful to swing over the back, and he couldn't stand on it to lift his good leg. He settled for laying across the bike and, very ungracefully and painfully, manoeuvred into position.

The bike started and purred into life, and he smiled faintly behind his visor. His leg had to be dragged into position onto the foot brake. Then he wormed his way out of the trees and back across the fields behind him.

The discomfort of his leg eased with the pressure of the bandage. Applying the rear brake with his leg became easier, but his head leaked blood into his eye, and the helmet prevented him from wiping it away.

Before rejoining the road at a small break in the hedgerow, Harvey stopped and pulled a plastic water bottle from the bike's panniers. He removed the helmet and cleaned his face up, before ripping his other shirt sleeve off and placing it over his head. The rest of the water he poured onto his leg wound, which stung badly, but felt better. He hadn't severed his femoral artery, but it was a nasty gash that would need to be cleaned. That could wait until after he'd finished with Donny.

16

PIGS MAY FLY

THERE WAS SILENCE. THE WORLD MOVED IN SLOW MOTION. Melody saw the cigarette being flicked from Roger's hand. It spun through the air like a firework and hit the ground at the front of the truck. The pool of fuel ran in a small but steady stream less than a foot from the burning ember.

A soft breeze, which would have been welcomed at almost any other time, gently rocked the trees on the edge of the fields, and prickled rather than stroked Melody's skin, and rolled the cigarette into the fuel.

The vapour caught the fiery end of the cigarette before the Marlboro even reached the liquid. The rush of flames popped into life like a magic trick.

Roger gazed down at Melody from the cab of the truck, he smiled the smile of a man who had won.

Melody turned and ran. She jumped from the road onto the embankment and plowed into Denver who was sending people back into the fields. They both tumbled down the unkempt grass over rocks. They landed together with a bump, in a drainage ditch at the bottom of the small hill when the flame found its way into the source of the fuel, and the tanker exploded.

A searing fireball reached out, reached up and licked everything in its reach, before mushrooming into an ungodly black cloud. The noise was deafening.

Melody and Denver turned their backs, the angle of the embankment protected them but they felt the heat wash over them. The flames rushed past just metres away.

Immediately the crowds began to scream, children started crying again, but the people were safely in the fields, spectating. They watched as their cars and vans were engulfed in the giant fireball. The closest cars caught alight and joined in the blaze. Possessions were lost, but lives had been saved.

A coolness came over Melody and Denver, and when they opened their eyes and glanced around, the land around them had been scorched to smoky and charred tufts of grass. The pair rose and ran back into the fields to a safer distance. The blaze was strong, the surrounding cars would likely explode when the pressure built inside their fuel tanks.

Melody and Denver made towards the large crowd who stood huddled together like frightened livestock. One man began to clap his hands as Denver and Melody reached safety. He was joined by another, and soon the chorus of applause increased as the whole crowd began to softly clap their hands in gratitude. There were no happy expressions, none of the joy that would typically accompany such a moment. It was just a sombre demonstration of appreciation.

"Is everybody okay?" Melody called to the crowd, her hands held high to get their attention. "Is anybody hurt?"

"Is anybody missing?" Denver followed.

The crowd shook their heads and held their families tight. Small groups of husbands, wives and children stood in contact with each other, touching. A few men stood alone, and one woman. They'd been travelling alone and now joined other people who had been travelling alone.

"Where's Reg?" asked Denver.

They both turned to face the blaze. Thick smoke poured from the vehicles and ran above the motorway like a locomotive had passed through, undeterred by the traffic that stood motionless. There was another crowd of people stood on the motorway itself, much further along than the blast.

"You think he's there?" said Melody.

"I didn't actually see him get out the van," said Denver.

They ran to the VW that Denver had stopped just fifty yards into the field. The single window in the back had been smashed by the truck, but the van had thankfully not been hit by the fireball. They peered into the windows, but Reg couldn't be seen. Melody wrenched the rear door open, and Reg's limp body began to roll off the van's wooden floor. Denver caught his arms before he hit the ground and pushed him back up.

He had a serious head wound, which had leaked blood across his face and pooled on the wood. A lump had formed on his forehead the size of a child's fist. Sirens in the distance kicked Melody into action. She pulled out her phone and dialled emergency services, stepping away from the van to talk to them.

Denver pulled the first aid kit from under the driver seat. He straightened Reg out and began to clean the wound, wiping the blood from his head and face. He used an open water bottle from the floor and his t-shirt to clean Reg's eyes before the blood dried and glued them shut.

Reg had a pulse, and his airways were clear so Denver made a pillow for his head. He put it in a position where the fresh blood that leaked from the wound ran away from Reg's eyes and face. Denver began to check for breaks and foreign objects. He started with his head, worked down his shoulders, just running his hands across his skeletal frame. Most fractures would be felt through the body's thin skin membrane. His ribs were intact, and Denver began to ease any thoughts of serious damage. Broken ribs often tore into lungs, or caused internal bleeding, which was a common cause of death. A first aider had no way of spotting early signs of internal bleeding.

Melody joined him once she had made the call. Denver was just finishing checking Reg's legs.

"No sign of broken bones or internal bleeding, just the bump on his head," said Denver. "His spine feels okay, but let's keep him straight until the medics arrive." He began to apply a field dressing from the van's first aid kit to the head wound.

Two fire trucks made their way along the hard shoulder, and seemingly without words, they sprung into action. Each of the firefighters expertly performed their own part of the effort to ready the hoses, build the pressure, and keep the crowds away, who had since moved closer out of curiosity. The distant thump of a helicopter nearing came over the empty fields, then the bird emerged from the smoke, and began to circle. The pilot brought the helicopter down into the field, a few hundred feet from the van.

The helicopter was yellow with a green underside. Essex Air Ambulance was written in large green letters across both sides.

Denver stood with his feet together and his arms up to form the letter Y, the international sign for help.

The first medic saw him and pointed his partner in their direction. Two men in green uniforms ran the short distance carrying a stretcher between them and an emergency medical pack.

"Thank god you're here, he's been out cold for..." Melody thought about how long it had been since Denver had avoided the queue of traffic and hurled the van off-road, "ten minutes, maybe fifteen."

"He's hit his head and has a large bump and a gash on his forehead. I've checked for broken bones, and his spine feels okay,' began Denver. "He nearly fell from the van when we opened the door, so we straightened him out, that's the only time he's been moved."

"Good, thanks, what's his name?" asked the medic. He was a middle-aged man, with greying and thinning hair, but he had a kind face. He pulled on a pair of latex gloves and checked Reg's eyes and airways.

"Reg Tenant, twenty-seven I think," said Melody.

"And are you his friends?" asked the man.

"Yeah, we're colleagues, but we're close."

"Can you tell me what happened here please?" the second medic asked, pointing back to the blaze with a jerk of his thumb. He was younger than the first guy, with a full head of neat brown hair in a side parting. Melody thought he couldn't be too long out of training but still had a confident way about him.

"The cars in front slammed on their brakes, we had no time, so I pulled off the road," said Denver.

The medic looked behind him and turned back to Denver with raised eyebrows.

"The truck behind us crashed into the tanker."

"Seems like a bad day for driving," said the younger medic. "There's another crash about a mile in front this one. Apparently, someone smashed into the car in the next lane on purpose and then took off. Caused a hell of a smash."

"Did they catch him?" asked Melody.

"Not that I heard, there was a family in the car that was hit. Crashed into the central reservation and rolled. There's another chopper there now dealing with the scene."

"Any description?" asked Melody.

"We don't get descriptions like that, miss. We just pick up the pieces."

"Right, let's get him onto the stretcher," interrupted the older medic. He'd finished his assessment. "Okay, Reg, we're going to move you now if you can hear me. Let me know if you feel anything."

Melody and Denver stood back and let the two men carefully ease Reg from the van onto the stretcher. The older man signalled the helicopter pilot, and the blades began to turn slowly.

"Can we come with him?" asked Melody.

"There's not much room," said the younger man, taking the back end of the stretcher.

"That's okay, I want to be with him."

Denver shut the rear door and pulled the keys. "I'll join you in a second."

"Need to be quick, this man needs a hospital."

"Get him loaded," said Denver. Without looking back, he ran to the nearest policeman who was a hundred yards away. He was asking a man in a suit questions. The man had obviously lost his car in the blaze and was giving his account of what happened.

"The insurance *will* cover it right? It's my livelihood, mate," he was saying when Denver came to a stop beside them.

"You'll need to deal with the insurance company, sir," replied the policeman.

"Sir," began Denver, "I need a word in your ear."

"I'm conducting an interview, sir. You'll need to wait, there's a lot of you to get through I'm afraid." He turned back to the man in the suit.

Denver pulled his ID, something he didn't like to do. "Officer, I said I need a word in your ear."

"Oh, I see. I'll just be a moment, sir," he said to the man, who then gave a look of annoyance at the disruption.

"That's my van in the field, we're with SO10. Our colleague was hurt, we're escorting him to hospital. I need the van protected." Denver passed him the keys.

"I'm afraid I-"

"The van is full of highly sensitive equipment and key information in a high profile investigation. If we lose the van or the contents, the suspects go free, and it'll be you, officer, that shoulders the blame." Denver made it clear he was reading the number on the policeman's shoulder.

"I'll see what I can do."

"You'll do more than that, you'll get the van into a police compound with twenty-four seven protection. I'll be back to get it later, officer." Denver spat the last words, and the policeman understood.

Denver turned and ran to the chopper as Melody was climbing in, she looked back and held the door for him. He climbed in beside her and pulled the door closed. The medic passed him a headset. Reg was on the stretcher at their feet, and the two medics were opposite monitoring his vitals. A strap ran across Reg's chest to keep his body steady.

The helicopter rose in the air, and Melody looked out of the small window at the devastation below. The scene looked even worse from above. They flew over the long queue of cars following the smoke, and saw the emergency services dealing with the cause of the traffic. Three cars were piled up blocking the motorway. The first vehicle was a minivan on its roof. Even from two hundred metres above, Melody could see the sparks made by the firefighters' cutting tools.

They passed, and she sat back. "Which hospital are we going to?" she asked into the headset.

"Broomfield Accident and Emergency," the medic replied.

She looked down at Reg. He looked peaceful. She thought that if the positions were changed, and she lay on the stretcher, Reg would probably be making jokes, and annoying the medics.

Reg opened his eyes and looked up at the ceiling, his neck brace prevented him moving his head. He tried to move his arms, but the straps held him fast. A confused look spread across his face, then a bolt of pain as his head began to pound. The medic held his head. "Mr Tenant, you're okay. You're in an air ambulance. Your friends are here with me, they're okay, but you've had a nasty bump on your head."

Reg tried to sit up, but the medic held him down.

"Reg, try not to move, can you hear me?"

Reg mouthed something inaudible.

"Okay, Mr Tenant,' the medic shouted over the noise, "I need you to move your fingers for me." Both hands and his fingers contracted and straightened.

"And your toes, Mr Tenant." Melody put her hands on his feet and nodded to the medic that his toes were moving.

"Okay, do you have any pain anywhere other than your head?"

He tried to move his head from side to side, then said, "No," softly and kept his eyes closed.

"Okay, you're going to be just fine. Just relax and try to stay awake. I'm going to keep talking, I want you to keep responding. I can't let you fall asleep."

Melody gently took hold of his hand. "Reg, it's me." She gave a little squeeze. He returned the squeeze. "That's it, Reg, just keep squeezing, hard as you can if you like."

Reg gave a soft squeeze. He lay on his back, totally disabled. His eyes were looking down at melody. She smiled back at him.

She held his gaze as the helicopter circled the helipad and turned to face the wind, then the pilot gently set the bird down. The rotors began to wind down immediately, and the medics jumped into action.

The doors were flung open, and the older medic jumped down. In one smooth motion, he pulled the stretcher out, and the younger guy followed with the other end. The legs were kicked down, and the stretcher rolled across to the open door where a team of men and women in white jackets stood to meet them.

Denver held Melody back with his arm.

"What are you doing?"

"Just wait," he said.

The pilot emerged, and Denver pulled his phone out. He nodded and said thanks to the pilot as he walked by. "Just making a quick call to his wife, We'll be in in a sec."

The pilot nodded and carried on walking. Denver watched him disappear through the doors.

"Come on," he said and ran toward the helicopter.

"What are you doing?" Melody called. But Denver was already pulling open the pilot's door. He climbed in and waved her over through the window.

She opened the passenger door at the front and looked across at him sternly. "We are not stealing a helicopter," she said matter of factly.

"We're not stealing it, we're borrowing it. Come on." He began to flick switches and familiarise himself with the controls.

"Denver, no. This is ridiculous, we could lose our jobs."

He stopped and faced her. "If we don't, we're out of the game. Murray gets away, more girls die." The rotors began to turn once more.

"Denver, no. I can't."

"Melody, Reg is in safe hands here. Get in." He took on a serious look. "More girls will die if he gets away. He'll just find another Cartwright someplace."

Melody glanced back over her shoulder then begrudgingly climbed in. "You better know what you're doing in this thing," she said, pulling on the headset.

Denver began talking through his own headset. He readout the helicopter's identifier to control. "Control this is Essex and Herts Air Ambulance KO-33, come back."

A crackled voice came over their headsets, "KO-33 this is control, who is this?" The control centre knew the regular pilots and hadn't recognised Denver's voice.

"My name is Denver Cox, I am a pilot with SO10, we have just dropped our colleague here at Broomfield and I am commandeering this helicopter in pursuit of a suspect. Out."

"KO-33, you can't do that. I suggest you step away from the helicopter before-"

"Control this KO-33, we don't have time for that, I suggest you ask your superiors to contact SO10, they'll verify my authority."

"KO-33, this is control, what's your flight plan?"

"Pudding Lane, Hainault, Essex. Out."

He switched channels back to the private channel so he could hear Melody's shouting.

"What the hell was that?" she shouted. He'd never seen her so mad. "That's it, we won't just lose our jobs, we'll go to prison ourselves you idiot. Why did you have to tell them who we were?"

"I couldn't lie to them, Melody."

"You couldn't bloody lie?" she shouted. A little spittle flew from her lip. "You can steal a helicopter, but you can't lie?" She released her strap and reached for the handle, but Denver took the weight of the chopper on the rotors, and it began to move. He eased off, taking the bird higher than the surrounding buildings, then checked the compass in the centre of the dials and banked.

Melody fastened her straps again. "You bastard," she called.

Denver smiled. "Sit back, enjoy the ride. How often do we get to do this?"

"Go to prison?"

Denver ignored her and monitored the controls. He checked the fuel, temperatures and pressure. Then sat back and looked out.

"Murray has a forty-five-minute head start on us, he'll be there by now, I'll cut across country."

"I'm not happy about this, Denver."

"Listen, if we get him, they'll thank us. If we don't, and we land ourselves in deep-"

"If?" cried Melody.

"If it happens, I'll take one hundred percent of the blame. I'll tell them I forced you into the chopper."

"Damn right you will." She crossed her arms and turned away from him.

"Melody, we can do this, but I need your help. Put that to one side right now and focus." He paused, then leaned over to her and held her arm. "We stand a much better chance of success if we work together, trust me, I can fly this, we can nail him."

"How long?" she said.

"At a guess, fifteen minutes."

"We'll probably be shot down by then anyway," she said.

17

THE HARDER THEY FALL

THE COLD WIND BIT INTO THE SCRAPES ON HARVEY'S HAND caused by punching through the plaster. His head throbbed, and his leg ached. He couldn't remember the last time his body had taken so many hits.

He rode for the sake of riding, to distance himself from the crime, the blaze, and the bodies, but he had no idea where to find Donny.

A chopper hovered back in the direction of the fire. It seemed to hang in the air swathed in smoke.

Harvey rode away from the blaze and continued along the country lane. He'd need to go back to basics, back to before he had the team with Reg's tech, Denver's reliability and Melody's tenacity and attention to detail.

Before he knew them he'd done all his own spadework, often sat alone at his kitchen counter on his laptop. He thought it all seemed so basic then, but he'd got the job done, whatever it happened to be. Often it had been researching known sex offenders to target so he could hone his skills. It had been therapy. Piecing the puzzle together, tracking their movements, until he managed to have them fall into his trap.

Then little by little, he could restore some kind peace to the world by removing some of the poison.

Another little part of Hannah could rest.

Another family could begin the long healing process.

Harvey had never been to see a shrink or a therapist, or whatever they were called. He often wondered what they might think of him if he began to tell them his story. Where would he start?

Would he start with Hannah?

Or would he start when his training had begun with Julios? That was when the world Harvey knew had been born. The real Harvey. The little boy that was found wrapped in a hamper on a bench seat in a grimy bar in East London had died when Hannah had cut herself to ribbons. Julios had reached inside the boy's corpse and pulled out a man, kicking and screaming at first. Harvey had wanted to fight the world and all those that deserved to be punished. But Julios has tamed the beast. He'd focused Harvey's attention on a small subset of evil. Now, he was a psychiatrist's dream.

And now Harvey needed to refocus. He needed to concentrate on one tiny part of the greater evil. Donny. One man. Harvey imagined a pin pricked into his own skin, relentless, its pressure unchanged. He imagined his life without the sharp stab of pain. How clearly he would see the world.

If he was Donny, where would he be? What would he do?

Donny would need to move quickly, he'd need to find a new place. It would be close. It had been less than a day. Nobody could find somewhere and move a bunch of girls and all that tech in less than a day. It would take a week to sign the lease. Unless he had friends. But what friends are going to lend him a commercial property for his illegal prostitution business? Besides, Donny had only one true friend, and Harvey had boiled him alive six months ago.

He pulled into a lay-by to remove his helmet and wipe his

face. Adjusting the make-shift bandage, he tidied up his leg dressing. His hand stung, but they were just scrapes. It had been a long few days, and he hadn't slept.

A lorry trundled by, heavy and cumbersome in the country lane. Harvey hung the helmet on his handlebars and leaned forwards. He was able to stretch his leg now, it hurt but felt good to move it. It would be dark soon, maybe an hour, maybe less.

Harvey ran the possibilities over in his head.

Donny would need to get the girls out fast. He'd need somewhere to take them and some way of taking them there. He couldn't take them in his car or Bruno's Toyota. He'd hire a lorry, he would have to, and he could do that in less than an hour. Once he had them out, he could take as long as he needed to find somewhere.

Harvey sat forward on his bike. Where would he park a lorry full of girls? He couldn't leave them alone at night, someone might find them. He'd have to kill them. If he set them free, they could go to the police. The description of a man in the area with a burned face and an accomplice that resembled a five-hundred-pound silverback would be easy for the police to track down. A caravan park? A campsite maybe?

Cogs shifted into place.

His foster father's old house. It was close by and had been derelict since Sergio's murder.

John had disappeared soon after the Sergio incident. His accounts had been closed, and all communication had been through his lawyers. It was the lawyers who had closed the bars down, laid off staff and put the house up for sale. The price had dropped after six months on the market, nobody wanted it. The news had been national. A man had been brutally killed there, and a known sex offender was found tied up in the basement. Nobody would buy the place.

Harvey fired up the bike and pulled his helmet on.

Harvey was closer to Loughton than Theydon Bois and decided to make a pass by Donny's apartment before riding on to the house. It was early evening, the streets were busy with people heading home from work and kids returning from school. He took a glance up at the building, and found the window where Donny's flat was. The lights were off in the corner of the second floor.

Harvey parked the bike in the same spot he had before and stashed his helmet in the back box. His Sig was in his waistband, his knife was fixed to his belt.

As he turned the corner near the ramp to the car park, a couple walked out the main door. He held it open for them so the husband could get the pushchair out.

"Thank you," the man said.

"You're welcome," Harvey replied with a friendly smile, then walked into the lift lobby. He was sure Donny wouldn't be there. Donny wouldn't be back. He knew the rules, never return to the scene. As far as Donny was concerned, he had caught Melody but still had no idea what organisation, if any, she belonged to. Barnaby had disappeared, and who knows what level of communication he'd had with Murray since Harvey had shot at his boat and Melody had been dragged from the water.

Donny would be moving. John may not have been the world's greatest father, he hadn't sat with them and helped with Donny's homework, but he had taught them to be street savvy. As weak and spineless as Donny had been when they were younger, he had picked up on that, and he had gone on to become John's operations manager across his chain of bars.

The door to the apartment stood at the end of the hall. Harvey saw the cleaning cupboard where he'd hidden before had been locked. He stood off to one side of the door and placed his finger over the spy hole, then rang the bell. He had his knife in his right hand, ready to jab up into somebody's throat if the door was to open. But it didn't.

The door was light oak, it was solid and intricately decorated with beading and an ornate design, like a fleur de lis symbol, but with more branches of interweaving plants.

The door lock cracked with a well-placed heel of Harvey's boot. He pushed it open. No movement. Harvey closed the door behind him. He swept each room before settling in Donny's bedroom. Donny had few possessions. The apartment looked like it was rented and came furnished. None of the furniture was Donny's style, it wasn't extravagant or expensive enough.

Double glass doors off the bedroom led out onto a small balcony with a table and chairs for two people. Harvey pulled the drawers out of a cabinet, there was no point being discreet. He emptied the contents of each drawer onto the bed. He didn't know what he was looking for, a clue to John perhaps. A clue to another property. But there were no clues in the bedroom.

He moved into the lounge. It was small, save for two large sofas and a small dining table for four. The drawers in the TV stand were empty.

It was like Donny had no previous life. He just rocked up at the place with nothing; a fresh start.

It had been a fresh start. Donny had been sent away when Thomson had put a hit on him and failed. John sent him off to the Maldives. Most people would've found somewhere a little cheaper, and with more people. Some places are easier to hide in, like Asia; India or Thailand would have been better choices. Donny didn't think like that. Sitting on an island with only a handful of other guests would have been his way of hiding. He must have returned from the Maldives when the calls from Sergio had stopped, and his money had run out. Donny would have found John's empty house. Harvey wondered if John had contacted him. John was the one link to Harvey's real parents, he would be the next piece of Harvey's life puzzle once he'd dealt with Donny.

The kitchen was empty. Harvey took a cursory glance around the apartment as he stepped to the front door, it had been a waste of time. He had gleaned an insight into what Donny had become. A nobody. Donny wouldn't live like that by choice. It meant he hadn't the money or position to splash out on a lavish home.

A single door stood behind the front door. Storage for a vacuum or ironing board perhaps. Harvey swung it open. It was dark inside, but it did indeed have an ironing board, plus some boxes for electrical appliances; the iron, microwave, toaster and kettle.

And a small rucksack stuffed at the back.

Harvey reached for the pack and unzipped the top. Inside were old photos. They hadn't been neatly stored or placed in the bag like cherished memories. They had been slung inside in a hurry. Some of the photos were bent in half. Some were in frames, most weren't. Harvey recognised a framed photo that had stood on John's bedside. It was of six people. John and Barb, Donny, Harvey and Hannah. Hannah was in a child's swimming costume, and Harvey was in shorts with wet hair. Donny was fully dressed. He never joined Harvey and Hannah even in the pool. Julios was stood off to one side. Harvey looked down at Julios' unsmiling face. His hands were folded in front of him. On guard. The photo was taken during the days before Harvey's training, when Julios had been John's minder.

Harvey faintly remembered the day. It was a shot of the family and, to an onlooker, gave the impression of happy memories of them by their pool during a summer long ago. In reality, Barb had spent the day sitting in a chair nearby, reading a book. John had been working in his office and Donny had been off with some outside friends. It was Julios who had spent the day with Harvey and Hannah, entertaining them. But it was John and Barb who had enjoyed the family photo. So people could see how happy they all were. Harvey looked again at Julois' unsmiling face and began to understand more.

He touched the photo. "One day my friend," he said to himself, "one day I'll find out who killed you. For sure I will."

Harvey zipped up the pack and pulled it over both shoulders. He glanced around the room, then opened the front door, and a large fist hit him square in the face.

The blow sent Harvey staggering back into the apartment, and onto the floor. He scrambled to his feet. The doorway was filled with the giant frame of Bruno; he was silhouetted against the bright hallway lights.

Bruno came at him with hard and fast jabs. Harvey ducked and slammed a hard uppercut into the big man's ribs with no effect.

Harvey had fought men as big as Bruno before. Their organs were protected by a layer of muscle and fat which narrowed the points of vulnerability down to the face, groin and throat. Many men Harvey had fought had placed a kick between the legs, thinking it would surely take any man down. But Harvey knew otherwise. A cheap shot between the legs would leave him open, standing on one leg, fully exposed and off-balance.

Bruno swung, Harvey dodged and felt the air move across his cheek. Bruno was fast for a big man. Perhaps not as much as most boxers, but the guy was still fast.

Bruno threw two more punches in quick succession, the first was a left jab anticipating Harvey to move into the follow up right hook. Harvey stepped back and let both punches miss. A missed punch takes a lot of energy and sets a man off-balance. Harvey was learning how Bruno fought before he made his move. Patience, planning and execution.

Bruno rushed at him, leaving no room to dodge, but Harvey ducked beneath his sweeping arms and stood with his back to the front door. Bruno grew mad. It was exactly what Harvey had been waiting for.

Bruno threw three wild swings at Harvey who was able to dodge, duck and skip out of their way. Harvey bounced from foot to foot, ready to move in any direction at any moment. Bruno ended up by the dining table and hurled two chairs at Harvey, who was again able to avoid the attack. But Bruno came at him while he moved from the last chair. He caught Harvey in his strong hands and pinned him against the wall. His breath was foul. Harvey landed several blows into Bruno's gut, but the giant man just laughed and squeezed tighter.

Harvey tried to pull at the man's huge fingers, but they were solid.

Bruno was trained and had learned the hard way how to street fight. His body was turned away to protect his groin.

Harvey felt his air supply being cut off. Bruno saw the life draining from Harvey's eyes.

Then he made his mistake.

He gloated.

Bruno put his face next to Harvey's and sneered, then in his deep East London accent grumbled, "Any message for your brother, Stone?"

In a fraction of a second Harvey snapped his mouth open and chomped his teeth on the big man's nose, he bit down with everything. But Bruno didn't let go. Harvey felt his own teeth sink into Bruno's skin, the irony taste of blood ran across his lips and down his face. He bit harder, growling, and twisting until finally his teeth connected; he'd bitten completely through. Harvey snatched his head back to tear the flesh clean from Bruno's face and spat it at him. Bruno was clearly in pain, his eyes were drawn tight and his mouth closed against the blood, yet he somehow managed to hold Harvey against the wall. He was almost inhuman. Bruno opened his eyes, and swung his arm back. A blow from him from such close range would have destroyed Harvey, it would be like a sledgehammer breaking his skull open.

Harvey saw the opportunity and jabbed his right hand up and out, fingers straight and locked. They connected with Bruno's adam's apple, and Bruno immediately released his grip. The larger man reached up to his own throat gasping for air. He fell to his knees, eyes wide. Blood poured from his ruined nose.

Harvey delivered the final blow.

18

STRUNG UP

DENVER FOLLOWED THE SMOKE.

"Well, he did say he would torch the place."

"You think the girls are out?" asked Melody. "Surely he wouldn't burn them all alive, it would link straight back to him."

"You're right, he'll take them someplace else to kill them," said Denver. "Someplace he thinks nobody will find."

Denver took the helicopter above Pudding Lane as they made their approach.

"That's Murray's car, on the grass," said Melody.

"Who's that down there? That's not Harvey."

It was an impressive scene. Two cars were on their roofs, one of them was Murray's, the other unknown. The barn was burning ferociously, pumping out thick, black smoke across the driveway. Murray was crouched behind the second car, and was shooting towards the end of the driveway, where another man was crouched down. The man shot, ran a few steps forwards, then crouched and shot again. At the end of the driveway, parked in the lane was a dark Volvo estate.

"Is that-"

"Frank," finished Melody. "Get me down there."

Denver pushed the cyclic forwards and lowered the collective. The helicopter surged and dropped down to fifty feet, where Denver levelled off.

"Denver, over there, take me down."

Denver continued on his path straight towards Murray.

"What are you doing?" cried Melody. "Take me down."

"Hold on, I've got an idea."

Denver brought the air ambulance in to hover directly above Murray and the upturned BMW. He dropped the collective some more, and the helicopter began to slowly descend.

Two gunshots pinged off the fuselage.

"We're going to get shot in the-"

"Trust me," shouted Denver, his face had a look of total concentration and steely determination.

Dust and smoke flew up all around them, Denver was pulling in the thick smoke through the suck of the chopper blades and sending it down onto Murray along with dust and debris.

"I can't see anything," called Melody.

"Neither can Murray,' said Denver, "it'll give Frank a chance to get closer."

Denver continued the onslaught of smoke and dust, and made small adjustments on the collective. Then he saw a faint Frank-shaped figure disappear under the helicopter.

Denver gently dabbed the right yaw pedal, and the fuselage turned to face the driveway. Then he slowly pulled up on the collective, bringing them out of the dust and smoke.

He moved the helicopter away from the fire and began to bring the chopper down on the driveway itself when he saw two fire trucks pulling in. He pulled the collective and took them back up out of the firefighters' way.

The smoke and dust had cleared around the upturned car,

and Frank had one knee on Murray's back putting cuffs on him.

"I'd say that was quite successful, wouldn't you?" Denver said with a smile.

"Who's is the other car?" asked Melody. "There's no-one around."

"Harvey," replied Denver.

"How can you be so sure?"

"That's an eighties BMW," Denver called over the radio. "If I had to steal a fast car in a short amount of time, I'd of chosen the same."

"You think he's in the barn or the car still?"

"Neither, he's a survivor. Besides, he has another mission."

"Cartwright."

"What about Frank?" asked Denver.

"We should talk to him, he'll be happy with the arrest so now's a good a time as any."

Denver brought the helicopter down softly beside the driveway. Police had arrived, and an ambulance had also turned up. The scene was a riot of swirling lights in the fading darkness. The rotors wound down and spun to a standstill.

They watched Frank hand Murray over to a uniformed officer, then turn to walk toward the chopper.

Melody opened her door and stepped down to the ground. It felt solid, sturdy and reassuring in comparison to the roller coaster chopper ride.

She called out to Frank as he approached, "You got the source."

"The *source*?"

"Yeah, *that's* Murray, *he's* the guy bringing the girls in."

"You have proof of that?"

"In a way, we were hoping for something stronger, but–"

"*I've* got him for attempted murder of a police officer."

"That'll buy us time to pull the human trafficking evidence together."

Frank looked across at Denver who was still sat in the pilot's seat. "Let's discuss the elephant in the room shall we?" he smiled. "Or should I say the helicopter in the crime scene?"

"Commandeered, sir."

"Commandeered?"

"From Broomfield."

"How do they feel about their helicopter being commandeered?"

"I'm sure they'll feel better when they hear about it being used to capture the leader of a human trafficking-"

"So they know who took it?"

"Of course, sir. Do I look like a helicopter thief?" Denver said with a smile.

"Cox, you were brought into the rehab program as a habitual car thief."

"That's just it, sir."

"What's it?"

"I'm rehabilitated. I turned my powers into good."

Frank turned away from Denver and looked down at Melody. "You have an update for me I hope?"

"It's bad, sir. Worse than we thought. Cartwright was in a gang of three running an illegal prostitution racket-"

"Are there *any* legal ones?"

"They *were* killing them, sir. Shaw wasn't the first or the last."

"The others?"

"With Cartwright? Barnaby Brayethwait and Jamie Creasey. We have Brayethwait in custody in Redbridge."

"How long do we have him for?"

"Life, sir. We have an audio confession placing Cartwright and Creasey in the spotlight too."

"Where's Creasey?"

"We planted a chip, but without Reg, we have no way of knowing where she is."

"Where's Tenant?"

"Reg is in Broomfield, sir. Head injury."

"Head injury?" Frank was beginning to wonder what the hell had been going on.

"Yes, sir. From the crash."

"What crash?"

"Murray's man rammed us in a truck, we came off the A12 and ditched in a field."

"Where's Murray's man now?"

"Burned, sir. He's dead."

"Burned?"

"In the explosion."

"*Explosion?*"

"Petrol tanker, sir. The truck rammed right into it. We evacced the public, no collateral."

"And Stone?"

"He left us, sir. On the coast."

"The coast?"

"We caught Murray and his man dropping off more girls. Followed them back to somewhere near Ipswich."

"Want some intel?" asked Frank.

"On what, sir?"

"Stone."

"You know where he is?"

"He crawled out of the BMW and ran into the barn." Melody looked across at the blaze, the crumpled old building had been reduced to a pile of burned timbers.

"Did he come out?"

"Nobody came out," Frank sighed.

"He was one of *us*, I thought *you'd* be little more upset," said Melody.

"He had one foot in," Frank defended. "He ran out on us. Stone was going to prison, and he damn well knew it."

Melody was hit hard with the news. Frank carried on talking, but she just heard a mumble of emotionless dribble. Around her, the firefighters were dousing the remnants of the old barn, blue lights flashed atop police cars at the end of the driveway, and police officers had begun a sweep search of the property.

"Mills," said Frank.

She looked up teary eyed.

"Sir."

"We just need Cartwright. You in? We can talk about Stone when we're done."

"Sir, I hope you don't me saying-"

"Go on."

"You're a cold bastard, sir." She looked passed him. A police officer was carrying Sneaky-Peeky toward his colleagues who were stood at the rear of a patrol car. They all looked at it with confusion.

"Denver, Sneaky-Peeky."

"What's-" began Frank, but Melody had already begun to walk across the grass toward them.

She returned two minutes later with the radio control tank and set it down on the ground.

"One of Reg's creation I presume?"

"Yes, we may have some footage on here that would secure Murray's conviction. We just need Cartwright, then as soon as Reg is up and on his feet we can scoop Creasey up." She looked up at Frank. "Cartwright either locked the girls in the barn and Murray has killed them, or Cartwright's taken them somewhere else. He's had about twelve hours so far to find a new place to run the operations from."

"Twelve hours? That's not a lot of time. I doubt he'd even get to see a place let alone sign a lease."

"Does he have friends nearby?"

"All the Cartwright allies went with John, his dad. The scene's been quiet for months." Frank thought on it. "He'd need a truck or a van right? To move all the girls I mean."

"Yes, sir."

"So presumably he'd need somewhere to park the truck overnight. It'd be too risky to park it on the side of a road somewhere."

The barn was, by then, reduced a pile of old burned, smoking timbers. "Let's have a quick look around, there's something I want to see," said Melody. She hoped there were no bodies. If there were, then they'd be charred beyond recognition.

They left Sneaky-Peeky sitting on the ground by the helicopter, and the three of them walked towards the smoking remains of the barn.

"There were two double doors here and single there." Melody pointed, but the doors were completely gone, and fallen timbers lay in their place.

"What's that?" said Frank, looking through the smoke. A pile of wooden timbers lay across something unmovable. Yellow paint was just visible in the grim blackness of the scene. Water from the firefighters, who were still dousing the barn, landed in a jet around the tall pile. Frank motioned for the firefighters to hold off for a second.

"That's a digger, sir," said Denver.

"A digger?" said Frank. "What did...." It dawned on him why they would need a digger. "Oh god, no."

"We saw it being driven out of the barn and around here," Melody said, as she walked behind the barn. She could still feel the heat of the burned wood, but the fire was entirely out. The stink was unbearable.

She looked around her. It was the spot where Bruno had

caught her. She remembered the soft earth but had only seen it in the dark before.

"Hey," she called to the firefighters, "you guys have spades?"

"Yeah, sure we do." A firefighter was stood waiting to continue dousing the fire.

"Think you can get us some?"

He called over his radio, and two shovels were brought across by a man with broad shoulders and black smeared across his face.

"Thank you, sir," said Melody. She took the shovels and passed one to Denver. She began to dig.

"Hey, we can do that for you,' said the firefighter.

"No, it's okay. In fact, I think it's best we clear this area."

"Are we okay to carry on now?"

"Yeah sure, thanks for your help," said Frank. He turned to Melody. "Is this going to be what I think it's going to be?"

"We didn't have eyes back here, but look at the soil. It's freshly dug." There were four freshly dug areas. They stood at the one furthest from the barn. Melody presumed it was the first.

She began to dig carefully. Denver joined in.

Within twenty minutes, they saw a hint of blue come through the dirt. The smell of decaying flesh was stronger than the stench of the burnt barn. Melody gagged.

"Okay no more," said Frank. "We're going to need forensics on this. Get the local unit to tape the whole area off, and get it guarded. I'll talk to the chief." Frank began to walk away.

Melody's phone buzzed in her pocket. She pulled it out and saw a message from an unknown number. The message read, *Gift, Aptmt 204, Loughton Heights*.

"Sir, it's Harvey," said Melody. She smiled broadly. "He's alive."

"Stone?" Frank's mind ran through various scenarios. "Follow me." They walked away from the smoky graves towards the driveway where Frank's car was parked.

"Where is he?" Frank asked.

"I don't know where he is now, but he's left us a gift, looks like Cartwright's apartment."

"You think it's Cartwright?"

"No, sir. That won't be a gift."

"Okay, get this place sealed off, and get a local cop to drive you down there. Denver, make the arrangements to have that chopper picked up please, so it can actually be used to go rescue people." He climbed into his car and started the engine. "I have an idea of where Cartwright might be, I'll call you if it works out."

Frank nosed his Volvo into the driveway of John Cartwright's old house in Theydon Bois. It was fifteen minutes from the farm in Pudding Lane and would be an ideal place for Donald Cartwright to keep a truckload of illegally imported prostitutes while he sought a new venue for his despicable enterprise.

The long gravel driveway remained as Frank remembered it. The grass was unkempt and covered in leaves. When Frank had last been there, the lawns had been immaculate. The little groundsman's house near the entrance, which was where Harvey had lived, had been a delightful little cottage. The gardener had maintained the appearance as it was the first structure a visitor saw when entering the gates. When Frank had last been there, a man had also been boiled to death in the basement.

Kids had since smashed the windows and spray painted graffiti on the door during its six months of being derelict.

The media had reported the property as being the scene of horrendous crimes, which made it a highly undesirable for potential buyers, and a magnet for kids looking for a place to hang out.

Frank saw no rented truck at the front of the house, so he pulled in and drove slowly up the smooth gravel driveway. He parked by the few steps that led up to the two huge front doors.

The right-hand door had been left ajar. No doubt from the same vandal kids that had broken the windows of Harvey's little cottage.

Frank unholstered his weapon and moved slowly inside. The house was deathly quiet and eerie. The door creaked when he pushed it open. Frank stood waiting for the noise to settle. Inside the great hallway stood two staircases, one on either side of the room, each leading up to the first floor in long winding arcs. Between the staircases was the doorway to the kitchen. On either side of the hallway was a room, each a mirror image in size and shape.

Frank had been in John Cartwright's office before. He had stood alone in there and smelled the history of the Cartwright family's business plans, fueled by brandy and cigarettes.

Frank wasn't interested in those two rooms. He stepped onto the hallway's parquet flooring and walked slowly and quietly between the grand staircases into the kitchen. The door to his right was closed. It was the door to the basement.

Frank pictured the scene he had found six months previous. He had walked down the stone steps slowly with his weapon raised at it was now. The cast iron claw feet of the antique bathtub had come into view. A warm damp smell of steam had hit him halfway down the steps.

The tub had begun to show itself as Frank descended the steps. It had been a large copper tub with several gas burners placed underneath it to boil the water. Far more than was necessary to heat a bath.

Then he'd seen the hand. His initial reaction was that somebody was indeed taking a bath, but the hand was unnaturally red and fixed in a tight, gripping position.

Sergio's pained death had been etched on his wrinkled face.

Frank opened the door and listened. Hushed whispers silenced in the darkness below at the sound of the door. He pulled his flashlight from his jacket but kept it turned off, his gun was in his other hand poised ready to fire. He stepped down one more step then turned to check the door was still open.

The sole of a boot caught him directly in his nose, and he tumbled down the hard stairs onto the concrete floor below. His torch rolled off into the darkness, and his weapon was gone, he'd dropped it on the stairs.

He lay in the darkness and heard the footsteps grow closer on the stairs. Slow, deliberate steps. It was the steps of a man who had all the time in the world. Frank heard the tone of the footsteps change as they reached the concrete floor.

The basement was pitch black. Frank silently fumbled for his weapon but all he found was the cold hard floor. He searched behind him and grabbed a naked foot, which flinched away at his touch with an audible gasp from somewhere above him. He crawled on his hands and knees away from the foot and the whispered gasp and was met with a hard blow to his face.

He spat blood and searched frantically around for the source of the attack, but the dark was so pure, there was no variance in shades. Just blackness.

He reached for his phone and pulled it from his pocket, but as soon as he hit the home button and the screen lit up, it was kicked from his hand. The phone scattered across the concrete floor and fell dark. Frank was sure his fingers had broken.

"Cartwright," he growled. "You're not making this any easier on-"

Another blow to his face. He felt his jaw move sideways, and he crumpled to the floor. The metallic tastes of adrenaline and blood mixed in the back of his throat; he panted with anxiety but forced himself to try and stand.

A boot stood on his back and slammed him to the floor. He spat and sucked in the dust and stale air, his lips lay on the dirty concrete.

Hands tugged at his arms, he felt the bind of zip-ties, and the bite of the plastic on his skin. He heard two of them being tightened, but his hands had lost sensation, he could no longer trust his senses. The darkness, the fall and the blows had disturbed his balance. His ears rang, or was it the sound of silence? His eyes saw only the darkness.

A harsh white light flickered then burst on, filling the room with clinical white light and blinding Frank. He squinted but saw nothing. Hands dragged him across the room and pulled him to his knees. Then they pulled a rough and scratchy manila rope over Frank's head. Somewhere close by they pulled the rope tight and Frank was forced to his feet then up on his toes, gasping for breath.

He tried to talk but the rope cut deeper, and his jaw shot pain into the side of his face from the kick. He growled with fear and fury.

Frank's vision settled and he opened his eyes. His sight focused on the wooden beam that his rope had been passed over, just like Sergio's had been. It was the same beam. The tight rope prevented Frank from looking down, but he could see many other ropes along the adjacent beam. He tried to count, but couldn't, it was too much. Thin slender wrists and limp hands were bound to the ceiling joints opposite him. He was central to them. More than ten, perhaps twelve, pairs of bound hands hung in the air at the bottom of Frank's eyesight.

"You remember this place?"

"Of course I do," he rasped.

"I grew up here you know. This house. So many memories."

Frank thought of the room. Hannah. Sergio. Shaun.

"I used to play down here if it was raining outside. Cook used to bring me my lunch, and I'd play with my toys. I remember my train set, it was spread across three big long tables. Those things are a work of art, you know? The detail was incredible. I had a mountain with a tunnel, trees and grass-"

"Sounds great, what every boy dreams of I'm sure."

"Some of us dreamed of bigger things than train sets," said Cartwright. "Some of us dreamed of not having to share our families with scum like my foster brother and his little slag of a sister." Cartwright over-pronounced the Ts in the sentence.

"So you were lonely?"

"No, not lonely."

"And Harvey?" asked Frank. "Wouldn't he play with you?" Frank was buying time.

"No, I wouldn't let him. He'd go off with *Hannah*. They had their *own* games. Childish games"

"You were older though weren't you?" asked Frank. "Didn't you *have* friends?"

"I still am older, wiser perhaps," grinned Donny. Frank heard the grin in his voice. "I'm still Harvey's big brother you know."

"I'm sorry to say, Donald," Frank used Cartwright's first name, he was easing him in. It was like the late night knocks on the doors of crying mothers and wives he'd had to do when he was starting in the force, "your brother was killed in the fire. There was nothing we could do."

"What fire?" said Donny. "I don't believe a word you say. I'm not falling for-"

"Murray burned the barn down, your barn Donald." Frank was drawing him in. "Smell my clothes, you can still smell the fire. The old wood went up in seconds. Took less than an hour for it to be burned to a pile of-"

"I don't believe you," snapped Donny. "Keep your mouth shut, pig. Why would Harvey be there anyway?"

Frank forced a laugh. "You won't get away with it, Donald. The police are on their way." The rope bit tighter into Franks' throat, and the last words trailed off.

"The police aren't coming, you came alone, didn't you? You wanted the bust for yourself. Couldn't resist it could you?" Donny raised a handgun to Frank's temple. "I'll make it quick. As you can see, I have a lot of work to do tonight."

"Is that the best you can do?" said Frank. "A bullet to the head? Your brother was far more imaginative."

Donny slammed his fist into Frank's gut. The older man sucked air in through his teeth, as much as his constrained throat would allow. "You want imaginative? Why don't I show you how imaginative I can be?"

A gunshot sounded, it was loud in the closed room. A chorus of muffled screams began.

"Quiet!" shouted Donny and aimed the weapon at another girl. The girls were immediately quiet, only their heavy breathing could be heard.

"Is that imaginative enough for you?"

"I can't see what it is you've done, Donald. Why don't you tell me what you did."

The rope went slack, and Frank dropped to the floor. The noose was still tight around his neck, but he gulped in air while he still could. Frank saw in front of him, the line of naked girls, the hands he'd seen. They had been bound by the wrists and hung from their bindings to the ceiling joist. Frank counted twelve girls. At the far right of the line, the last girl's head slumped forwards, and thick gloopy blood dripped down her body to the floor beneath her.

"One down," said Donny cruelly.

"How many rounds do you have left?"

"Enough," said Donny. "Do you like what you see? Pretty aren't they?"

The girls were all below twenty years old and trim. Two of them looked almost starved, Frank could clearly see their ribs. They had all been bound and gagged.

"You want to see some more?"

"If you stop now, I'll see to it that you're looked after."

"*Looked after?*" Donny screwed his face up.

"Inside, you'll *go* to prison for sure, I can't stop *that*, but I *can* make sure you're looked after inside, you'll be comfortable."

Donny laughed bitterly. "Is *that* supposed to entice me?" Donny breathed and composed himself. "You'll need to do better than that, old man." He paused. "What's your name?"

"Me?"

"Of course you. What's your name?"

"It's Frank. My name's Frank."

"Ah, you look like a Frank." Cartwright moved towards the girls in front of Frank and turned back to him. "This one's my favourite, Frank," he said, and ran his hand along the inside of the girl's leg. She twitched and squirmed but couldn't move away. Tears began to roll down her face. He traced the outline of her ribs with his fingers, softly and slowly, and then her breasts which were full and firm. He took one in his hand.

"People pay a lot of money for this, Frank. Her skin is so

soft," he traced the outline of the girl's nipple, "and she smells so," he searched for the scent with his nose, "feminine," he finished. "Ahhhh."

"Let her be, you sick son of a bitch." Frank looked away.

"I thought you wanted me to be more imaginative, Frank. How am I doing?"

Frank turned back slowly, he knew it, but his eyes confirmed. Donny gently nuzzled the barrel of his gun between the girl's legs. He smiled at Frank whose eyes had begun to run. Then Cartwright turned the gun upwards.

"What do you say, Franky?" Donny hissed. "Creative?"

"You're sick, take it away."

The girl's bladder released and a thin stream of liquid that ran down her legs. It pooled beneath her, so Donny stepped away.

"She's dirty now, but it's okay, we have spare."

"Is it worth it, Donald?"

"Donny," said Cartwright. "Call me Donny. All my friends do."

"You have friends?" asked Frank.

"Some."

"I thought your brother boiled your only friend?"

Donny was silent.

"Sergio," began Frank, "yeah, he was a coward too, wasn't he? No wonder you got on so well."

Donny stepped away from the girl and yanked on the rope. Frank was dragged to his feet once more. The rope bit into his throat.

"What do you know about Sergio?" asked Donny. He raised the gun to Frank's forehead.

"I was the unfortunate bastard that found him," said Frank, "right where I'm standing."

"Found him?"

"He was taking a bath. Didn't you hear about that?"

"Sergio was dead long before I came home," said Cartwright.

"Oh, so you aren't aware of Harvey's last great act then?"

"His last great act?"

"He works for me now, did you know?"

"You lie, he would *never* work for the police-"

"Truth," cut in Frank. "He *came* to *me*." Frank paused, then spoke calmly and softly, "and do you want to hear something very special?"

"Special?" said Cartwright.

"Special," replied Frank. "He *knows*."

"He knows *what?*"

"He knows your *secret*."

"*What* secret?"

"The one you and Sergio were hiding all this time. All those years, with sleepless nights wondering what he'd do if he found out."

"We didn't have *any* secrets, Harvey knows nothing."

"Your father told him a few home truths, and I have to say, it certainly explains all this." Frank gestured at the girls. "You're sick and perverted, Donald. You need locking up."

Cartwright looked interested. "*What* home truths?"

"Let's just say that John Cartwright let slip about Sergio raping Harvey's sister."

Donny inhaled through his nose.

"Harvey brought Sergio down here. It's almost ironic that you hung me from this beam. It's the very same one as... well, you know?"

"As what?"

"The one Sergio was hung from."

"He hung Sergio?"

"No, not properly, that was just to stop the little weasel running away, Donald. Much like you've done to me."

Frank paused, timing his next sentence just right.

"Harvey boiled Sergio alive."

Donny looked distraught and incredulous, "He did what?"

"Remember the old copper bathtub that was here?"

Donny did, he glanced around for it.

"The police took it away a long time ago, Donald. Evidence. See what I mean by his imagination? He's so much more *creative* in his work."

Donny was silent.

"Like I said, Donald. I had the misfortune to be the one who found him, Sergio that is." Frank moved his neck in the tight scratchy noose. "His skin was peeling off."

"Stop it."

"His eyes had even boiled white, I'd never seen that before."

"Shut up."

"He was all puffed up like a balloon. Thought he'd pop we did."

"Lies."

"Truth, Donald. Truth." Frank softened his voice. "I heard the recording."

"What recording?"

"The one Harvey made."

Donny looked at Frank questioningly.

"Harvey recorded it all you see. I found the dictaphone on the little table over there."

Donny turned to see the table, it was covered in dust.

"You want to know what Sergio's last words were?"

"No," said Donny. His mouth had an upturned grimace of pure hatred. "I want to know what yours will be." Donny raised the gun and stepped back.

"He cried of course, like a child," Frank continued, ignoring Cartwright.

"He was weak," said Cartwright.

"Yes, he was, Donald. He wailed and sobbed. Will you cry?"

"When?"

"When Harvey comes for *you?*"

"You said he was dead."

"Lies, Donald." Frank was running out of time. "His last words, Sergio's. You want to *know* what he said?" Frank spat. "You want to know what Sergio told Harvey as he hung right here from bound hands, with the boiling water waiting below, ready to take him, to swallow him and cleanse him of his sins?"

"No."

"You *should* know."

"Don't say it."

"He was your friend?"

"I'll kill you *right* now." Cartwright's hands trembled.

"It was Donny."

Donny stepped back further.

"You hear me, Donald?"

"You're filth. You lie."

"He's been hunting *you*, Donald," hissed Frank. "*You're* the last one on his list."

"No, I know things, things he'll want to know. He won't be able to kill me," said Cartwright, almost convincing himself. "He'll need me alive, I have the answers to his parents and Julios, I'm the only left who knows about Julios' mistake. I'm the only one who knows about Adeo."

"The reason he was sent away?"

"You know about that?"

"I've been around a long time, Donald."

"It doesn't matter, the secret dies with us both."

"Oh, I don't know about that, Donald. But you know what I do know?" Frank smiled.

"What?" Cartwright was breathing heavy, Frank had wound him up like a clockwork toy. He'd been easy.

The lights went out.

The basement was plunged into darkness once more. The girls all gave a harmony of stifled whimpers.

"*He's here*," whispered Frank. Cartwright heard the grin in Frank's voice.

19

FEEDING TIME

DONNY PANICKED. FRANK SAW THE LOOK OF TERROR IN HIS eyes. He knew Harvey and what he was capable of.

"I know it's you, Harvey," shouted Donny up the stairs, "you come down here and I'll kill them all. Every one of them."

Frank heard Donny's frantic breathing.

"You hear me?"

Harvey didn't reply.

"Answer me you coward."

Harvey didn't reply.

"There's no escape, Donald," said Frank softly. "Stone, it's Frank," he shouted as loudly as he could with the restricting rope around his neck, "don't come down here. Donald is going to lay his weapon down and untie me. I'll bring him up to you, and you will not harm him."

Silence.

"That's it," said Cartwright. He moved towards Frank and roughly pulled the noose from his neck. Frank stood and rolled his head, freeing up the tension that had built.

Frank felt the gun on the back of his head.

"Move." Cartwright's voice had become cold, but scared.

Frank stepped cautiously to the stairs in the darkness. "Harvey, I'm coming up, don't shoot me."

He took the steps slowly, the gun never lost contact with his skull.

They reached the top of the stairs, and Frank turned left into the main hallway.

"Harvey, it's us, we're coming out," shouted Frank.

"Shut up, you're a hostage," hissed Cartwright. "Walk faster."

Frank picked up the pace just a little and strode into the hallway. Both front doors stood wide open, and leaves scattered the floor. It felt like days since Frank had walked through there.

"Stop."

Frank stopped.

"Harvey, where are you?" called Cartwright. "Don't cock about."

The soft stringed introduction of an orchestral tune that Cartwright recognised faded gently into the room, coming from John Cartwright's old office.

Cartwright turned sharply at the sound as it grew in body, strength and warmth. The cellos began to add their weight to the ensemble. Frank felt them through the wooden parquet floor.

"I know it's you, Harvey. Show yourself," shouted Cartwright. The music grew louder still.

Cartwright shoved Frank forwards, who turned and looked him up and down.

"Open the office door," said Cartwright, "don't do anything stupid."

Frank stepped over to the door. With each slow step across the huge hallway, Frank expected the blow to his back.

It didn't come.

He reached the door, turned his back to fumble with his bound wrists and awkwardly gripped the doorknob. Frank turned it and pushed it open, before stepping clear of the door. He faced Cartwright, who stood with his gun raised at the empty doorway. He was visibly shaking; the gun moved in his hands.

With the door open, the music rang out clearer. The intensity increased with every phrase, every bar and every beat.

Violins straddled the soprano and tenor rhythm and danced delicate melodies through the ever-increasing baritone body the cellos sung.

The crisp string tones ran from the empty room through the open door and danced their way to freedom and beyond, through the front door and up the winding stairs where great paintings had once hung majestically. Sad-looking, empty spaces now stained the yellowing walls, as the only memory of the paintings that had been sold off separately. They now hung on foreign walls, in some happier place.

"Harvey!" shouted Cartwright. "Harvey! Stop playing games."

Frank stood motionless against the wall.

A loud thud came from the kitchen. Cartwright jerked his head, he was twitchy. He would snap soon.

"No. No!" shouted Cartwright, his voice rasped with fear. He stepped back away from the kitchen and towards the front doors.

The dead girl, number twelve, lay on the cold wooden floor at the top of the steps to the basement. She'd bled dry, but Frank could see the top of her head, shards of skull stood bright against the dark red insides.

Cartwright stepped closer to the girl's body. His head flicked back to Frank who stood still against the wall.

"Follow me," he said. Then called out again to Harvey.

"I know you're down there, Harvey."

Cartwright stepped across the body and rushed to the top of the stairs, his gun aimed into the darkness below. He fired off three shots into the shadows and stood waiting and watching for Harvey's body to slump to the floor.

Harvey didn't slump to the floor. He wasn't there.

Harvey waited in the shadows of the dimly lit kitchen. He sat in the place he had sat once before, a long time ago.

"I know you're down there, Harvey." Harvey heard Donny call out down the stairs. Then he heard him fire off three rounds that would hit the hard floor and ricochet off to nowhere.

Harvey stepped up silently behind the door and stood tall behind his foster brother. He reached back and drove the sharp end of his blade through Donny's knee cap. It was a move designed to immobilise the victim by destroying the cartilage and knee joint. Donny would never walk on two legs again. Donny screamed and reached down at the pain instinctively.

Harvey was ready and grabbed Donny's gun hand, twisting the weapon and his fingers.

Donny tried in vain to squeeze the trigger but couldn't move his twisted fingers. His ruined leg gave way, and he fell to the top step.

Harvey kicked out hard at the back of his foster brother's head, and Donny fell forwards, cracking his face against the concrete. He bounced from wall to wall and landed with a thud as his head gave a final bounce on the last step.

Frank walked slowly towards Harvey. He turned to show his bound and empty hands then stood by Harvey's side.

Frank noticed Harvey's discomfort, then the dark patch of blood and gaping hole in his cargo pants.

The two exchanged a glance but said nothing of the wound.

Frank peered down into the darkness then turned back towards the front door. Sirens wailed as police cars skidded across the tired lawn, and ground to a halt on the gravel driveway.

Harvey closed the basement door.

"It's over, Harvey," said Frank.

Harvey didn't reply.

"Where are *we*, Harvey?" said Frank. "Are you on your own?"

Harvey looked from the darkness into Frank's eyes.

"This needs finishing, Frank."

"And then what?"

"It's over."

"And what do I get?"

"You got Brayethwait?"

"Yeah."

"You got Murray?"

"I did."

"You have Creasey?"

"We can find her, she's chipped."

"You have the clients?"

"Apparently so, an unexpected bonus."

Harvey opened up the door wide and called down. "Come on, let's go."

A nervous head appeared at the foot of the stairs.

Harvey waved her up, "Come on, it's okay."

The first naked girl was joined by other girls, and they walked up the stairs together, but not like the scared children they had been, timid and afraid. They walked now with purpose, as a group, and with the confidence of women.

"You're setting them free? They're illegal immigrants."

"No, they're victims of human trafficking. I gifted them to you."

"Gifted?"

"Gifted, Frank. They'll identify Murray as the ringleader if you treat them right. You've got your case."

There was a silence as one by one, the girls emerged from the stairway. Harvey stepped back to allow them room. The first girl walked out, covering her nudity with bloodied hands. Harvey's eyes followed her as she stepped out into the hallway, and found Melody stood at the two great front doors. Harvey jerked his head in greeting. She stepped inside and took off her coat to cover the girl.

The rest followed slowly and shyly, each of them with their bloodied arms wrapped around themselves. Melody had them wait in the hallway, then took the coats of the uniformed policemen outside and gave each girl a jacket, before leading them out into the dark night. Flashing blue lights lit each one rhythmically as they were led down the steps to the warm, waiting police cars.

"How do we do this, Stone?"

Harvey didn't reply.

"We had a deal. You *stop* the killing, work *with* us, not *against* us, and you *don't* go to prison. You're putting me in a very difficult position."

"Donny raped my sister."

"I know, Stone. It must be hard to know that he's lying down there, and all you have to do is walk down those steps and finish the job."

Harvey didn't reply.

"Think about *this*, whatever mode of suffering you have in mind for Donny, whatever slow and painful death you're dreaming up, right now, it'll be the last one. The last person you'll ever stop. The last person you'll save." Frank stepped around the dead girl on the floor and made to walk out. "If you choose to do that, it's the end."

Frank turned and walked away. Harvey watched him leaving; he saw the blue lights lighting his long coat and greying hair.

"Carver."

Frank stopped and turned.

"Sometimes, people are *meant* to suffer. Sometimes, their sins are so great that a good man can't take another step in his life without knowing that he fulfilled that obligation when he had the chance. To make the sinner suffer, to help the sinner repent. It's an obligation to society, to those that fell because of him, and to those that, in some other circumstance, would fall at some other time, a month from now, a year, however long it is. We can't let these people walk the streets as free men."

"That's right, Stone. That's our job."

"But sometimes, Frank, it's those who have been wronged *themselves*, and have suffered at the hands of that monster, been humiliated, frightened and come close to death, that get that chance by some moral twist of fate. The chance to fulfil an obligation. And it's the victims that *deserve* that chance, Frank, more than anyone. They're the ones who *need* the opportunity, the chance to repay that suffering. The chance to walk free, knowing that the monster that once destroyed their lives suffered a cruel and painful death."

"What are you saying, Stone?"

"It's a balance, Frank."

Frank began to walk towards Harvey again.

"Do you understand, Frank?"

"I think I'm beginning to."

Frank looked down the dark staircase.

"Sometimes, Stone. A man who has a debt to pay needs to pay that debt to the people he owes."

"And sometimes, Frank, a man's vengeance is satiated from knowing that the debt was paid by someone who deserved it more."

Frank looked back at the cars waiting outside. Pale faces stared from the windows, ghostly in the night. He turned back to Harvey.

"If we go down there, what will we find?"

"A debt repaid."

"And who repaid the debt?"

Harvey glanced back at the police cars outside; pale, scared faces stared back at him.

"Those who were owed. Those that were obligated and had suffered the most."

20

COLLATERAL

FRANK STOOD IN THE OPEN-SHUTTER DOOR OF HIS UNIT'S HQ. The smell of the Thames was strong, and the cold morning breeze whipped between the building and the perimeter wall.

The first vehicle was arriving. It was Melody, of course, in her little sports car. A coffee in her hand, she climbed out the car and smiled.

"Good morning, sir."

He returned the smile. "Good morning, Mills. One of these days, you'll bring *me* one of those."

"One of these days you'll ask nicely." She stood beside him.

"You have a report for me, Mills?"

"I'll type it up first thing. It was a late night, sir."

"You have an informal report?"

"On the case? We got them, sir."

"We did, how about the team?"

"The team, sir?"

"I've been here since two am, Mills, and you know what I've been doing?" Frank was standing tall, his hands deep inside the pockets of his long jacket; his breath fell away in clouds.

"Writing reports, sir?"

"No, I've been gathering other people's reports, Mills."

"Sir?"

"Two stolen boats?"

"Ah."

"One stolen BMW?"

"That was Harvey, sir."

"A stolen *helicopter*?"

"Not really stolen, sir. Commandeered."

"Do you know how many cars were written off in the fireball on the A12? The fireball you lot caused."

Melody puffed her cheeks then exhaled. "A few, sir."

"Nine, Mills. Nine cars written off. More were damaged of course. And then there's the tanker full of petrol, not to mention the VW."

"Ah, yeah that's going to need–"

"Throwing in the river, Mills, that's what that's going to need."

Another engine drew nearer, and Harvey's bike turned the corner.

"Oh thank god for small mercies," said Frank under his breath. Harvey rode past them and parked his bike inside beside the tools. Frank and Melody watched him remove his helmet and hang it on the handlebars.

He strode over to join them in the doorway.

"Stone," said Frank in greeting.

"Frank."

Melody just smiled at him. Harvey raised an eyebrow at her in return.

"Sleep well, Stone?" said Frank without turning to face him."

"I didn't sleep yet."

Melody turned to him. "It's been days, Harvey, you must be shattered."

"I'll grab some rest when this is over."

"It *is* over, we did it, Stone."

"Not the job, Frank."

"What then?"

"The bollocking, Frank."

"The bollocking?"

Harvey didn't reply.

"There'll be no bollockings today, Stone. That I can assure you."

A loud engine approached with a scraping metallic sound.

The ruined VW Transporter trundled around the corner with Denver at the wheel, its exhaust dragged along the concrete floor beneath it. Frank, Melody and Harvey stepped out the way to let Denver past. He parked next to Harvey's bike.

"Morning team," said Denver as he stepped out the van carrying a coffee. "Got my own thanks, Melody."

"What? Am I supposed to supply the coffee now?" she said defensively.

Denver walked around with a skip in his step and opened the rear door. It needed a hard push to open fully as the rear of the van was smashed in from the impact with the truck. The shattered glass window had been replaced with a plastic sheet.

As the door opened, a friendly face appeared inside the van.

"Reg," cried Melody, "oh it's so good to see you." She hugged him as he climbed from the rear of the van.

"Welcome back, Tenant," said Frank, shaking his hand.

Reg turned to Harvey, and Harvey held out his hand. Reg pushed it away, then grinned and went in for a hug. Harvey was shocked but laughed and slapped his back.

"So you're all better? That was quick," said Melody as they walked towards the stairs for the debrief.

"No, I discharged myself. Had to sign some papers-"

"What? Why?"

"No internet, no TV, nothing. I woke up with a banging headache. Then waited four hours for a nurse to bring me something to eat." He pointed to the bandage. "I have to change this every day, and I'm not supposed to look at TV or screens."

"Yeah right," said Denver.

"I'll be okay. Severe concussion, they called it." He rattled a bottle of pills as he walked up the stairs. "But as long as I take these, I'll be okay."

"So you got airlifted out for a headache?" said Melody.

"And had a nap," said Reg, "I feel quite rested actually. So what's been going on here then?"

Melody turned to Harvey who was walking behind her.

"Oh, not much, Reg," said Melody. "Not much at all really."

Frank stood by the whiteboard at the head of the room. Reg and Denver were on the comfy couches. Melody sat at the small table facing Frank, and Harvey stood with his arms folded leaning against the wall by the door.

"Okay," began Frank, "the players?" He pulled the lid off his pen.

"Brayethwait," called Melody. Frank wrote *Brayethwait* on the board and then asked, "status?"

"Custody," replied Melody.

"Who caught him?"

"Harvey," said Melody.

"You put the cuffs on him," said Harvey.

"*You* didn't *kill* him," replied Melody.

"I presume there's a story behind that?"

"Erm yes, sir," said Melody, "along with the audio confession nailing Creasey and Cartwright."

"Good, I want that in your report. *Next?*"

"Creasey," said Denver.

"Status?"

The team looked at each other.

"She's chipped, sir."

"Tenant, I need you to find her on LUCY and coordinate with Essex Police."

"Yes, sir. First job."

"Next?"

"Cartwright," said Denver.

The room fell silent.

"Status?"

"Deceased," said Harvey.

Frank turned to Harvey, "How? For the report I mean."

"Repaid debt."

Frank nodded. Melody looked in wonder, she picked up on something between Frank and Harvey, something strong, a bond or understanding.

"Next?"

"Mason," replied Reg.

"Mason?" asked Frank. "Who's Mason?"

"Cartwright's minder, sir," said Melody.

"Status?"

"In custody," said Harvey.

"And a wheel chair for the rest of his life," finished Melody.

Frank raised his eyebrows and looked between Harvey and Melody.

"It'll be in-" began Melody.

"I'd suggest we leave the details out of that if need be," said Frank.

"Next?"

"Roger," said Denver.

"Roger?"

"Murray's accomplice."

"Status?"

"Deceased, sir."

"The fireball?"

"Yes, sir."

Frank wrote deceased next to Roger's name.

"Next?"

"Murray."

"Status?"

The team were silent.

"Aha, yes, that one was my bag. The big fish. My quarry." Frank looked smug. "Nice to know I can still bag 'em when my team's off stealing helicopters, boats and BMWs."

"Well done, sir," said Melody, smiling.

Frank wrote *In Custody*, beside Murray's name on the board.

"How many boats, helicopters or cars did *I* steal to catch him?" he asked.

The team didn't answer.

"How many explosions did I cause to catch him?"

Silence.

"Good, that's what I like to hear." He turned and smiled to let them know he was playing. "Okay, so hostages. We haven't had a hostage case for a while."

"Eleven girls were freed, sir," said Melody. "Saved."

"Good, reports from forensics say they found four bodies buried behind the farm. Plus one in the house, and it looks like the girls will point the finger at Murray for a free lift home to wherever it was they were from."

The team were smiling. Melody looked around her, they were a bunch of misfits, but she felt at home with them.

"Good work, team," added Frank. "I might add that, if we do plan on commandeering any mode of transport in the future, we run that decision by me beforehand? It'll save a lot of explanations."

"Yes, sir. We are sorry, sir," said Melody.

"What about Stokes and Narakimo?" said Harvey.

Frank raised an eyebrow and turned to Reg.

"Reg, can you-"

"Yes, sir. Work with the local units and bring them in."

"Thanks, team, that's not a bad result. Messy, but still a good result," said Frank, drawing a circle around the list of outcomes on the board. I want all your reports in by close of business."

Denver stood. "Sir," he began, "the VW, it's pretty much f-"

"We need a new van, Cox, do we?" Frank cut him off.

"Yes, sir."

"I might be able to help there." All eyes fell on Harvey, who lifted his rucksack from the floor and threw it to Frank.

Frank caught it and winced at his fingers that weren't broken but were still sore. He looked at Harvey questioningly.

"Should I be concerned?"

Harvey didn't reply.

Frank unzipped the zipper and looked inside. He tipped the contents of the bag onto the large table at the head of the room. Bundles of bank notes fell out the bag and piled high across the surface.

"How much?" asked Frank.

"Three hundred grand, give or take."

"Three hundred thousand pound?" Frank sounded surprised.

"Give or take."

Frank paused, then, "Stone, can you take a walk with me?"
Frank began to bundle to cash back into the rucksack.

"Do I have a choice?"

"Stone," replied Frank, "haven't I always given you choices?"

21

DEAL WITH THE DEVIL

THEY STOOD SIDE BY SIDE AND LEANED ON THE RAILING beside the river. The air was frigid and Frank's jacket flapped in the wind that ran across the choppy water.

"We had a good result," said Frank, "much of it was down to you I hear."

Harvey didn't reply.

"Your an asset, Stone, I want you on the team. You've come a long way. I want to take you further."

"Further?"

"From your past."

Harvey didn't reply.

"You had unanswered questions. Are they behind you now, Harvey?" It was the first time Frank had called Harvey by his first name.

"We all have questions, Frank."

"But *you* needed answers, some of us move on, some of us get over it."

"My sister killed herself, Frank. Did you *expect* me to move on and get over it?"

"No, part of me understands."

"Part of you?"

"My wife died three years ago. I still don't understand."

"I never knew."

"Nobody does," said Frank.

"What if you knew somebody out there had the answer? Would *you* look for it?"

"Maybe, Harvey. Maybe not. We had many years together, my wife and I. So many good times." Frank gazed across the water. "It took a long while for me to move on, to get over the bitterness and to enjoy life again."

"Do you enjoy life, Frank?"

"No, not really, but I appreciate what we had. It doesn't really matter what happened now or how she died or by whose hands, nobody can take those memories away from me. They're mine."

"We're all different."

"Yes, we are, aren't we? Especially you, Harvey. I've met some cold bastards in my time, ruthless killers."

"I probably knew them."

"You probably did, in fact, you probably killed some of them too in your past life."

"Maybe, I didn't make a list." The truth was that Harvey didn't need a list. He remembered the faces of them all.

"You have a quality, Harvey. You're a talented man, like I said, an asset. But you have this good within you. I've tried to find the word before, but there isn't one. You're not a bad person. People like a man who stands up for society's weaker members."

"I'm not sure where this is going, Frank. If you want me, I'm back on the team. But you need to take the noose off." The mention of the word noose sent vivid images of the basement into Frank's mind.

"Noose?"

"Yeah, noose. I *can't* have the threat of prison hanging

over me. You can't expect me to jump with both feet if my head's in the noose."

Frank sighed. "You're right. But I can't take the noose off until I *know* you've left your past behind, Harvey."

Harvey didn't reply.

"You still have questions, don't you? You're still seeking answers."

"My whole life has been a lie. One big web of deceit. How would you feel?"

"I'd feel angry I guess."

"I'm past angry, Frank."

"I understand."

"Do you? Where were born, Frank?"

"Near Edinburgh."

"And your parents?"

"Frank and Carol Carver."

"Are they alive still?"

"No, they died a *long* time ago, Harvey. They led a very quiet life. My father was a farmer, he didn't earn much, enough for them to get by."

"Old age?"

"Yes, peacefully in their sleep, both of them."

"Nice."

"You *could* call it that."

"What if somebody told you one day that all that was a lie? That everything you've ever been told about them had been a lie."

"What do you mean, Harvey?"

"There never *was* any Frank and Carol Carver near Edinburgh, and they *didn't* die peacefully in their sleep."

"I see."

"Do you?"

"You want the answers?"

"*I'll* find the answers, one way or another, Frank,"

"So the noose stays on does it?"

"If the noose stays on, I keep one foot out."

"What if I helped you?"

"Help me? Do what exactly"

"Find the answers, Harvey. *Us*, the *team*. We have the means. You have the motivation, as it were. I don't see why we can't do some digging. Might make it quicker." Frank turned to him, he stood two feet away. Harvey turned to face him.

"I don't want to be the one to remove the noose. But I'll help *you* remove the noose yourself. Like you said in the house, sometimes it's those who need to repay the debt that should be given the opportunity."

"And then the noose is gone?"

"And then the noose is gone."

"How do you plan on helping me? I've searched my entire life and just hit walls every step of the way."

"Well, not so long ago I had a noose around my own neck, Harvey. A man stood before me, as I stand in front of you now. He knew death approached, he heard the footsteps in the darkness." Frank's eyes softened. "In his frantic despair, and as death loomed over him, a tall and fearless figure, he spoke of your parents and the answers you seek."

Harvey didn't reply.

The End.

END OF BOOK STUFF

Stone Fall · Book Three · Chapter One

Two men sat in a black cab outside St Leonard's Primary School. The driver looked like any other black cab driver and took the same fare every day. He was dressed for comfort in trainers, a t-shirt and jogging bottoms, just like he did on most days. The other man sat in the large rear space with an open newspaper and flicked through the trashy photos of celebrities. He wore a pair of jeans and a loose jacket over an open-necked polo shirt.

All around them were mums and friends chatting while they waited to collect their children from school. The women stood in groups of two or three making idle small talk between glances at the front doors of the large brick building. They were waiting for the first opportunity to break away from the meaningless chat and get back home to their lives.

Among the mums were several men, not dads, but drivers, who stood unsmiling beside their cars. The school was private, well-regarded and extremely expensive.

The driver had parked a hundred yards back from the main gate, close enough for the little girl to see the cab, but far enough away from the eyes of prying mothers.

The main doors opened, and dozens of uniformed kids ran out towards the waiting arms of their mums. They showed pictures they had painted during class, some opened tupperware boxes to display the cakes they had baked and passed their mums their bags to carry for them. Other kids met their drivers and simply climbed into the back of the car without conversation.

"You'll never get away with this," said the driver to the man in the back. "She's just a kid."

"Relax, she is merely a pawn," said the man in the back seat, "just like your family, Mr Bell. I have no use for them, but sometimes we need a little..." he paused thoughtfully, "encouragement. I have far greater ambitions, Mr Bell, than anything to do with the lives of young children. I deal in nations. So much grander, don't you think?"

"But she won't recognise you, you'll scare her," the driver replied.

"Inshallah, by the time she opens the door it will be too late."

The intuition of the man in the rear paid off. A short while later the door was opened by a little girl, and she climbed in.

"Hey, who are you?" she said.

""Oh, you must be Angel?" said the man in the back. "It's okay, I am helping, Mr Bell today. Why don't you close the door, it's cold outside, yes?"

Angel turned and pulled the heavy door closed, before settling herself onto the seat.

"Do you need help with the seatbelt?"

"No, I can do it myself, I do it every day."

"Oh, well you must be a very clever girl then, Angel. Drive on."

The driver indicated, pulled away from the curb and joined the slow moving traffic.

"So," said the man in the back, "tell me about your day, Angel. Did you make a painting? Or cook a cake?"

"You don't make a painting, you paint a painting, and you don't cook a cake, you bake a cake."

The man laughed. "Such a clever girl, you know when I went to school, we didn't learn such things."

"Where did you go to school?"

"A long way from here, Angel. Somewhere very far away, but it is always in my heart, and I can find my way home with my eyes closed. Is this place in your heart, Angel?"

"My school?"

"Yes, your school, your friends and the city. Do you love them?"

"I love my friends, but not my school."

"And the city, Angel? Do you love London?"

"I don't know, I haven't been anywhere else, so I don't know what's better."

"You really are a very clever girl for somebody so young."

"How do you know how old I am?" Angel asked.

"Oh, Angel, we know all about you. And your Mum."

"Where are we going? This isn't the way."

"I must be honest with you, Angel, we are going for a little holiday. Perhaps afterwards you will know if you miss your home or not."

The man was busy pouring a liquid from a small plastic bottle onto a handkerchief.

"Where are we going? What's that you're doing?" asked Angel. "I want my mum."

"Little girl, you have asked too many questions. It's nap time."

ALSO BY J.D.WESTON.

The Stone Cold Thriller Series.

Book 1 - Stone Cold.

Book 2 - Stone Fury

Book 3 - Stone Fall

Book 4 - Stone Rage

Book 5 - Stone Free

Book 6 - Stone Game

Novellas

Stone Breed

Stone Blood (Available at the end of Stone Rage)

The Alaskan Adventure

Where the Mountains Kiss the Sun

From the Ocean to the Stream

.

APPRECIATION

If you enjoyed Stone Cold, please do help me to continue Harvey's story by leaving an honest review.

A few short lines about your experience with the book can be all it takes to help a future reader discover the series.

Many thanks.

J.D. Weston

To learn more about J.D. Weston

www.jdweston.com

john@jdweston.com

A NOTE FROM THE AUTHOR

The Stone Cold Thriller series is set in East London and Essex and features places from my own childhood.

While many of the buildings, pubs and streets are fictitious, some of the more prominent locations in the series are borne from my own life experience and are as accurate as my memory allows.

My family are from Theydon Bois, where John Cartwright's house is located. In fact, my parents lived in the great house before I was born, renting a room off the wealthy owner.

The headquarters building is based on the same road as my first flat in Silvertown, opposite London's City Airport.

In the first book, Stone Cold, the location of the first murder was in fact in the same building as my first job.

While the locations may offer an insight into my own childhood, and early working years, the characters are all fictitious. I recently handed the first draft of book one, Stone Cold to some family members and discovered that John Cartwright is, in fact, the name of my great-grandfather. I hope that he wasn't into the things the character John Cartwright is, and if he was, I'd like to know where the money went.

Stone Fury was an absolute pleasure to write. The places were all familiar in my mind, and the characters truly came to life. Melody, Reg and Denver played a much larger role in the story, and each character grew and developed organically with little guidance from me; all I did was type the words as the story unfolded.

I do hope you've enjoyed the series so far, but more than that, I hope you've grown to feel for Harvey and the other characters, and if you've come this far, perhaps you'll come a little further and see how the next part of Harvey's story unfolds. I wish I could tell you, I'm itching to just blurt it out. But hey, where's the fun in that?

J.D.Weston

To learn more about J.D.Weston

www.jdweston.com
john@jdweston.com

STONE COLD

Book One of the Stone Cold Thriller series

One priceless set of diamonds. Three of London's ruthless East End crime families. One very angry assassin with a hit list.

Harvey Stone has questions that someone will answer. Who killed his parents and why? Who raped and killed his sister? And why are his closest allies hiding the truth?

When Harvey is asked to kill East London's biggest crime boss in return for one name on his list, there is only one answer.

Can Harvey survive the gang war, untangle the web of deceit and uncover the truth behind his sister's death?

Stone Cold is the first book in the Stone Cold thriller series.

If you enjoy fast-paced adventure, gritty vigilante stories and no-nonsense heroes, then you'll love J.D. Weston's brand new Thriller Series.

Unlock the Stone Cold Thriller Series with the first book, Stone Cold.

STONE FURY

Book Two of the Stone Cold Thriller series

The lives of twelve young girls are being sold. The seller is on Harvey Stone's list.

When ex-hitman Harvey Stone learns of a human trafficking ring taking place in his old stomping ground, he is sickened. But when he learns the name of the person running the show, an opportunity arises to cross one more name of his list.

Can Harvey save the ill-fated girls, and serve justice to those who are most deserved?

Stone Fury is the second book in the Stone Cold thriller series.

If you enjoy fast-paced adventure, gritty vigilante stories and no-nonsense heroes, then you'll love J.D.Weston's brand new Thriller Series.

STONE FALL

Book Three of the Stone Cold Thriller series

One evil terrorist with a plan to change the face of London. One missing child, and one priceless jade Buddha. Only Harvey Stone and his team of organised crime specialists can prevent disaster.

When Harvey and the team intercept a heist to rob a priceless jade Buddha, little did they know they would be uncovering a terrorist attack on London's St Paul's Cathedral, and a shocking hostage scenario.

Can Harvey and the team stop the terrorists, save the little girl and rescue the priceless Buddha?

Stone Fall is the third book in the Stone Cold thriller series.

If you enjoy fast-paced adventure, gritty vigilante stories and no-nonsense heroes, then you'll love J.D. Weston's brand new Thriller Series.

Buy now to read the next adventure in the Stone Cold thriller series.

STONE RAGE

Book Four of the Stone Cold Thriller series

Two of east London's most notorious gangs go head to head with the Albanian mafia, and one angry assassin who's out to clean up.

When Harvey Stone is sent undercover to put a stop a turf war between the Albanian mafia and two of East London's most notorious gangs, nobody expected him to be welcomed like a hero by an old face.

Has Harvey finally gone rogue, or will he put a stop to the bloodshed once and for all?

Stone Rage is the fourth book in the Stone Cold thriller series.

If you enjoy fast-paced adventure, gritty vigilante stories and no-nonsense heroes, then you'll love J.D. Weston's brand new Thriller Series.

Buy now and get your hands on Harvey's next adventure in the Stone Cold thriller series.

Made in the USA
Lexington, KY
07 May 2018